DANGEROUS THAW

KARI LEE HARMON

look forward to reading what comes next in this series."--*Top Amazon Reviewer*

"If you enjoy a book with twists and turns, is suspenseful, has murder and mystery along with romance, this book is for you. I enjoyed the book from the first chapter until the last. I would recommend this book to anyone who enjoys action, adventure, strong women, dependability and loyalty, family, action, suspense, mystery, solving murder and, of course, romance. This is an exciting romance suspense book."--*Top Amazon Reviewer*

"This is my first book by Kari and let me tell you it will not be the last!!! Wow, so much intrigue, so many secrets. I usually read historical romance, or regency. This book will grab you with the first page. There are a lot of characters, and each has his or her own secrets and past. This book has so much mystery and suspense you just can't put it down. Just when you think you have figured it all out, wham the story takes a hard right and you're wrong!! Kari will have you guessing till the end. There is romance too but woven into the story. This is not a romance story; it is a mystery with lots of intrigue, twists, and turns. I can't wait to see what book two will be!! Rush to get your copy, but don't plan on getting anything else done until you finish it...enjoy."--*Top Amazon Reviewer*

"Harmon is a masterful storyteller who weaves together a fascinating tale of betrayal, redemption and love. The characters will captivate you. It is a phenomenal addition to the series."--*Top Amazon Reviewer*

"There are some wonderful characters and intense scenes. Emma and Gunner grow close and find a bond and lasting love as they solve the crime."— *Top Amazon Reviewer*

I enjoyed this excellent story and would recommend it to those who like stories with romance, mystery, and suspense. This tale is sure to keep you on the edge of your seat."-- *Top Amazon Reviewer*

Harmon's second book in her Coldwater Cove romantic suspense series is as interesting and fast-paced as the first one. It definitely kept me on my toes with its many twists and turns, danger, and possible suspects. It's a gripping tale that had me swiping pages as fast as I could, just to read what happens next. Emma had a few "what were you thinking" moments, and Gunner could have not let his past betrayal affect his present...but I loved the two of them together. Their chemistry and the heat from their smexytimes was off the charts. And Emma's Dream Team of JoJo and Harvey had me completely entertained. Then came the ending and I was blown away by who the mastermind was. An entertaining book from the first page until the last. I highly recommend this enthralling romantic suspense and look forward to the next book in the series. Each book stands alone, but I think you should read them all for maximum enjoyment."-- *Top Amazon Reviewer*

This is a new to me author and I LOVED the story. Loaded with angst and suspense, well developed characters and a non-stop story line, this book was a winner from the first to the last. Hard to put down. I started the series here and it does work as a standalone but it was good enough that I'll go pick up the previous book which I understand takes place in the same town."-- *Top Amazon Reviewer*

For all the women out there who have been mentally, emotionally, and physically abused, just know you're not alone. There is always someone ready to help, you just have to be brave enough to ask for it. This book is for all my girls who are brave, beautiful, smart, and strong.

Emily Townsend, Samara Townsend, Sam Wilks, and Ana Richardson
(Honorary shout-out to Meghan Russo--my niece who will always be one of my girls)

You girls fill my life with such joy. I hope you all know you are loved, and I will always be there for you no matter what. I am so proud of all of you for how much you have accomplished, and I can't wait to see what the future has in store for you. Never be afraid to follow your dreams and always remember to be kind to others. Love you most!

Love, Mom

ACKNOWLEDGMENTS

I would be remiss if I didn't give a special thank you to my fabulous editor, Alaina Crosby. She has such an amazing eye and knows exactly what it takes to make a book shine. Her feedback and suggestions are always exactly on point, especially for this book in particular. I am so lucky to have her as part of my team.

Thank you, Alaina! You rock!!!

Olivia Jones stood on the dock of Coldwater Cove in northern Maine, looking out over the water as she sipped her steaming cup of morning coffee. The Cove was a small, picturesque seaside fishing village with a humid continental climate. Direct strikes from hurricanes and tropical storms were rare this far north because of the cooler Atlantic waters, but severe nor'easters were possible between November and March.

That was what happened this past winter. A nor'easter hit The Cove, turning into a blizzard as it moved inland, breaking records. It was March and the snow was just starting to melt. Of course, Olivia had only heard about this from the news and the locals, having only moved to town a few days ago. She was renting the old Coswell Cottage that Sheriff Trent West had restored a while back.

The new realtor team, Johnson Family Finds, consisted of Tia, Calvin, and Dijon Johnson. Their family had expanded their Portland business with their children by opening an office in Coldwater Cove. Tia was the youngest of the siblings, eager to prove herself. The moment Olivia had arrived in town, Tia had offered to look for a house for her.

Tia was model tall with gorgeous caramel skin and buzzed blonde hair. She was chic and in the know, but Olivia wasn't sure how long she wanted to stay in the cove. In the meantime, the cottage suited her needs perfectly. It was right on the water, further down the coast from the marina, and the cabin next to her was empty. Close enough to civilization, yet far enough away to be left alone. It had been five years. She'd thought she had put it behind her, but recent events had brought everything back, making it feel like it was yesterday.

She needed to be alone after what had happened.

Everything she'd tried hadn't helped. After her thirty-fourth birthday recently, she knew she needed a change. Looking around the marina, she took in the rugged coastline with jagged rocks and forested slopes that swept down to the sea as if drowning the coast. While the cliffs were peppered with rocky shores dotted with lighthouses, peninsulas reached toward the sea like an old woman's hand, clawing at the waves.

Spring was bare and colorless, like Olivia's mood.

She inhaled a deep breath, smelling the salty air, fish, and seaweed. A hint of pine and smoke from someone's woodstove wafted past her nose, reminding her she wasn't alone. She'd come here for a fresh start. Soon enough flowers would bloom, and life would begin again. She was hoping maybe *her* life would begin again.

A dog barked further down the dock, sending a flock of gulls flying and squawking high in the sky. The rumble of a boat engine drew Olivia's eyes to vessels of various sizes that were moored against the docks, getting ready to start their day. Fishing boats had left the harbor hours ago, but the charter boats were waiting for the tourists to awaken. From everything Olivia had read, winters were always hard on The Cove, but spring breathed new life and money into the town.

As the new coroner, Olivia would be working closely with Sheriff West. She was actually a board-certified medical examiner who used to work in New York City, but the small town only had the budget to hire a coroner. She'd needed to get away to someplace remote, so she'd taken the job and hadn't looked back.

Trent's wife, Stacy, was a journalist, and she introduced Olivia to her best friend, Mayor Laura Flemming. While Stacy was Amazon tall, Laura was a petite dynamo who didn't let her size stop her. Olivia could relate. She was also petite but not nearly as gutsy. A pain twinged above her chest to the side, and her fingers fluttered to the spot. Pulling her hand away, she wrapped her palms around her mug, focusing on anything but the memories that threatened to flood her.

Laura was tough on crime, but fair and full of ideas to help grow the town, starting with hiring a talented event planner and his team to kick off the spring festivals. Maple Sunday was up first, followed by Spring Fest, then Moose Mania, and finally the Food, Wine, and Art Festival, which Olivia was most looking forward to.

"You're a hard woman to track down, Dr. Jones." Deputy Zoe Granger looked like the poster girl for Ms. Fitness Magazine as she came to a stop beside Olivia.

She wasn't a bulky, muscular woman, but she was extremely toned and fit, looking sharp in her traditional tan-and-brown uniform, complete with a tie, wide-brimmed hat, and low, platinum blonde bun riding beneath. She stared at Olivia with a serious, no-nonsense expression, waiting for a response.

"Sorry." Olivia chewed her bottom lip, not sure why she should feel uncomfortable. She certainly didn't do anything wrong, but the deputy was so intense. "I was just enjoying a cup of coffee before starting my day. There's something about the water that's always called to me. One of the main reasons why I moved here."

Deputy Granger's face lost its tough expression. "Same. I was in the Coast Guard for a while, but that didn't work out so well." She blinked as if surprised she'd shared that much. The features on her face pinched in a way Olivia recognized as she stared out over the water, her ice blue eyes becoming guarded once more. She clearly didn't want to talk about whatever she had been through.

Neither did Olivia.

"So, how can I help you?" She took a sip of her coffee, cradling the mug tighter to warm her hands. This far north, the winter's chill didn't want to loosen its grip too soon.

"Sheriff West and Mayor Flemming want to see you at your office, straight away." Deputy Granger nodded once, sharply.

The coroner's office and morgue were held in the same building as the crime lab and sheriff's office.

"I'll head there now. Thank you, Deputy." Olivia finished her coffee as the woman left, and then she went to work. That was what she was here for, after all. Starting over in a small, *safe* town.

She was done with big, dark, scary cities and the scars they left behind.

* * *

"DR. JONES." Sheriff West swept his hat from his head and reached out to shake Olivia's hand, his hazel eyes kind but serious as he stood outside her office.

She was used to observing things closely, paying attention to details. As sheriff, he was a level-headed, no-

nonsense, by-the-book kind of man. He was a bit intimidating in his uniform with his tall, muscular stature and the military-style buzz cut he sported. He'd married a fiery redhead with crazy curls, who complimented her husband well with her fun, outgoing personality. From what Olivia could tell, they were both good people.

"Sheriff." Oliva shook his hand and nodded once in response.

Folding her arms across her sweater, she fidgeted with the threads. She'd always been on the quiet side, but she was even more so these days. People in general made her uncomfortable. She turned to the woman beside him, who wore a smart, chic, lilac suit and heels that made Olivia feel even more awkward in her drab, boring, navy-blue slacks, light-gray sweater, loafers, and simple black braid that fell to her waist.

Laura smiled, waiting patiently.

Olivia cleared her throat. "How can I help you, Mayor Flemming?"

"You can start by calling me Laura." Her lavender eyes twinkled as she held out her hand. She was all of five-foot-two with a blonde pixie cut, yet judging by her reputation, people took her seriously.

That gave Oliva hope.

She was only five feet tall and terribly shy, especially around men. She released the tension from her shoulders and smiled back as she shook Laura's hand. "Only if you call me Olivia."

"Done. Shall we go inside to talk?"

"Sorry. Don't know where my manners went."

Olivia opened the door and led the way inside. Stale air wrinkled her nose, so she cracked a window open. The Sheriff and mayor both took a seat across from her battered desk, and she added it to her list of things to change asap.

"How do you like your new office?" Laura looked around the room, her smile slipping as though she was trying not to cringe.

"It's smaller than I'm used to," Olivia admitted, "but it will do just fine."

"Sorry about Clive's mess." Sheriff West rubbed his jaw and glanced at the multiple boxes full of files scattered around the room. "He was good at his job, but he wasn't very organized, unfortunately. He had a system only he knew how to decipher, and he passed away before he could rectify that." The Sheriff made the sign of the cross.

"I'm sorry to hear that." Olivia folded her hands in front of her.

"The man was in his eighties. A chain smoker who loved his scotch, but he wouldn't have it any other way. He died doing what he loved to do." Trent's lips tipped up slightly, and he shook his head.

When Olivia had first arrived in town a few days ago, this office had overwhelmed her. She'd only just started going through the boxes and creating her own file system. Thankfully, things were slow around here, because she had a feeling organizing this office was going to take a while.

"It's okay. I don't mind being busy."

The Sheriff eyed her curiously but didn't say anything.

"Well, there's nothing pressing at the moment, so you have time," Laura said. "I just wanted to check in and make sure you have everything you need."

"Don't hesitate to come to me or Deputy Granger if you have any questions or need anything at all."

"Thank you, Sheriff West. I appreciate that."

"You're welcome. We're all happy to have someone with your qualifications here. I have to say I was a little surprised you would want to come to such a small operation compared to the one you were at in New York City."

"Big cities aren't all they're cracked up to be, Sheriff." A shiver had Olivia pulling her sleeves over her hands as she added, "A small-town atmosphere is exactly what I need right now."

He nodded, tilting his head to the side. "How's the cottage, by the way?"

She felt her face transform into a genuine smile. "Amazing. You're very skilled at carpentry."

"So my wife keeps telling me." He grunted. "I fixed up her father's house after he moved in with his girlfriend, Doc Hurn. They're off sailing around the world, checking off items on their bucket list." He chuckled. "Now that the house has sold, my wife has me working on an addition to the colonial we bought."

"I can't blame her. What kind of addition?"

His eyes softened. "A nursery."

Olivia smiled. "Congratulations. You must be very excited."

"Thrilled and scared to death." He blew out a breath, then finally relaxed a little and smiled back. "You can call me Trent."

"Then you must call me Olivia."

"Well, we won't keep you any longer, Olivia." Laura stood. "I have a meeting with the event planner in thirty minutes. Our town is still recovering from the winter nor'easter, so I want these spring festivals to be fabulous. The more people who come to our cove, the more money we will have for the town. I intend to do her justice, like Mayor Buchannan wanted."

"Stacy's late mother used to be mayor a long time ago, and it was her mission to right the wrongs and put Coldwater Cove on the map," Trent explained. "Stacy and Laura have been trying to do that ever since, in her honor."

"How sweet. I would say they're doing a great job at that."

Olivia had read about Stacy's mother being murdered all those years ago, but the town's new website showed all the progress the town had made since then to clean up the streets and keep them safe. It was one of the reasons Olivia had chosen Coldwater Cove to relocate to. Small-town charm with friendly people and loads of possibilities.

Trent and Laura left, and Olivia got to work, feeling a sense of excitement and hope. Like nothing could possibly go wrong that day.

* * *

"I HEARD the chowder is fantastic here." Olivia hung her coat on the back of her chair and took a seat at the bar in The Claw.

"You heard right." The bartender winked, his dirty-blond wavy hair too long and his sea-green eyes twinkling. "Have we met before? You look really familiar."

She lowered her gaze out of a force of habit. "No, I'm new to town."

"Huh. Well, I guess everyone has a doubleganger." Her eyes met his as he was restocking glasses and already onto a different topic, thankfully. "The Claw is my family's restaurant. I live in the apartment upstairs and manage it, now that my parents have retired. I'm also a volunteer firefighter, and I run a snowplow business in the off season. The world-class chowder, however, is all my mother's doing."

"Deputy Granger recommended it."

"Zoe, huh?" His eyebrows puckered. "She's a tough one. I didn't expect that." He ran a hand through his wavey strands and smiled wide, revealing straight white teeth. "Give Granger a thank-you for me. Looks like I owe her one." He held out his hand. "Jack Ross."

The waterfront pub was located at the edge of the marina, where regulars like fishing boat captains and their crew hung out. It had a charming nautical theme, sporting local pictures of the catch of the day on the walls. The lighting was dim, providing a cozy ambiance, as classic rock filtered through the sound system. A reality TV fishing show played on the big screen above the bar.

Olivia shook his hand. "Olivia Jones."

"Ah, so you're the new coroner I've heard so much about."

"Medical examiner, actually."

He raised a brow. "Nice." He studied her as he wiped down the bar top. "How are you liking our fine town so far?"

"It's quiet. I like *that* a lot."

"Wait until the tourists start arriving." He chuckled, then his smiled slipped. "I'll take busy if it means more money for the town. This last storm nearly did us in."

"I watched it play out on the news. I'm just glad no one died."

His eyes flashed with pain for a brief moment, but then a proud expression crossed over his face. "Thanks to my sister, Emma, and her Dream Team of storm chasers, Harvey and JoJo, warning times and solutions to handle big storms are much better than they were in the past."

"Does your sister live local?"

"Nah, she's down the coast in Virginia with her Navy Seal boyfriend, Gunner, but it's okay. She's doing important work, and she promised to visit more often," he slapped the bar twice, punctuating his words, "so it's all good."

"That's nice." Olivia smiled wistfully. "I don't have

any family. It's just me." She was an only child and had been on her own since her parents died in a car crash while she was in college. She ran a hand down the chain around her neck to the large cross with her parents' names on each side that she always wore around her neck.

"It's not just you anymore. Now you have a whole town behind you." He poured a draft and slid it down the bar without missing a beat. "We look out for our own. Isn't that right, Eugene?"

Eugene caught the draft without spilling a drop and took a sip before replying, "Right as rain." He rubbed his leg. "Any moment now, anyway." The elderly man sitting a couple seats down from Olivia at the bar had a long white beard and a fishing cap, looking like the Old Man of the Sea.

"Your freezer's all set, Jack." A stocky man with a dark-brown beard and thick head of equally dark hair emerged from the kitchen, carrying a toolbox.

"Thanks, Larry. You're a lifesaver." Jack shook the man's hand, then glanced at Olivia. "This is Larry Shaw, Coldwater Cove's finest maintenance man yet. We were lucky to find him." The man's face flushed. "Larry, this is Dr. Jones, Coldwater Cove's new medical examiner. We were even luckier to find her."

"Please, call me Olivia." She held out her hand. "It's a pleasure to meet you."

Larry took her hand and bowed his head. "The pleasure is all mine, ma'am." He tipped his head to Jack. "Gotta run. I'm booked all day."

"See you, Larry." Jack waved and then turned his attention back on Olivia. "Can I get you a drink?"

"Just an iced tea. I'm still on the clock." Olivia looked at her watch.

She'd taken a break from tackling Clive's catastrophe of an office system and had gone out for lunch. It had been raining on and off since she'd arrived in town a few days ago, helping to thaw the ice and snow, but what a miserable slushy mess it had created.

"First one's on me. Welcome to town, Dr. Jones." Jack set the steaming bowl of New England clam chowder down with a basket of buttery rolls and a tossed side-salad.

She was proud of her degree but had always been uncomfortable with the awe-inspiring formality that came along with it. "*Olivia* is fine." Her mouth was already watering. "Thank you so much for this. I've been busy cleaning up my office and the lab. I guess I didn't realize just how hungry I was."

"I can only imagine." Jack half-grunted, half-laughed as he topped off her iced tea. "Clive Owen sure was a character."

She took the first bite of the rich soup, filled with tender potatoes and juicy lumps of clam swimming in a pool of thick cream, and her eyes rolled back in heaven. The rolls were light and fluffy, topped with a thick layer of buttery goodness that melted in her mouth after dipping them in the soup.

Jack raised a brow, waiting expectantly.

"Deputy Granger was wrong. This isn't good... it's fantastic!" Olivia blinked, surprising herself with her response. She normally said very little, but there was something about Coldwater Cove that was already helping her to relax. It felt like home.

Maybe she had finally found a place she wanted to stay.

Sirens started wailing at that moment in the marina, sending her heart to her throat. She hated sirens. Another reason she'd moved away from the city. The Claw grew quiet as everyone froze. Jack's scanner and phone went off simultaneously, but she couldn't make out what it said. Her eyes met his and suddenly everyone ran outside to see what was amiss.

Olivia spotted Sheriff West, Deputy Granger, and Mayor Flemming huddled together at the edge of the water with the harbormaster, Remy Finkelstein. He was a short, skinny man with curly red hair and glasses. Trent had introduced Olivia to the harbormaster when she'd first arrived. He'd replaced Charlie Wentworth when he retired, bringing youth and new energy to the harbor.

The rain was coming down in buckets now. Olivia pulled up the hood to her raincoat. She'd learned quickly to keep a raincoat and duck boots in her office. She'd switched to them before lunch, just in case. The weather in northern Maine could be so fickle, turning on a dime at any moment.

"Hey there Remy, Trent, Laura… Granger." Jack nodded, his gaze lingering on the deputy for a moment before traveling back to the Sheriff's. "I heard the details over my scanner. My father is coming to man the pub. I'm at your disposal." Jack had grabbed his volunteer firefighter gear he must keep in the pub, and carried it with him. He was donning it as he spoke.

"The rescue dive team should be here any minute. I'll go meet them," Remy said, heading in that direction.

"I'm sure the chief could use your help, too, Jack." Trent scanned the marina with a frown.

Half the town had arrived already. Olivia might be from a big city, but even she knew there was no keeping secrets in a small town. Jack gave him the thumbs-up and jogged after Remy to join the other volunteers who were arriving one by one. Deputy Granger caught up with him, most likely to add her former Coast Guard experience to whatever was happening.

"This is the worst possible timing." Laura pulled her umbrella down tighter to her head. "The Cove can't afford any more drama right before the spring festival season."

"You know the spring thaw can be dangerous in these parts," Trent pointed out. "Don't panic before we know what happened for sure."

"Can I help?" Olivia asked.

They both looked at her.

"More than you know," Laura said.

Oliva blinked. She still didn't know the details. "What on earth happened?"

"A dead body washed ashore a little while ago, and we need a coroner's report with the cause of death." Trent looked at her apologetically. "Guess The Cove isn't so quiet after all."

2

Olivia closed her eyes and strove to calm her nerves. A dead body her first week in town. The initial coroner's report would legally document who the deceased was, and determine the cause of death. Because the death occurred months ago in the winter and the body had clearly been preserved in the ice and snow, an autopsy was needed to determine the full extent of what had happened.

Luckily for Coldwater Cove, she was qualified to perform one.

Autopsies only took two to four hours to perform, with preliminary results released within twenty-four hours, but the full report could take up to six weeks to prepare. So much for tackling Clive's Catastrophe.

Olivia walked to the office down the hall and knocked on Trent's door.

"Come in," he said from inside the room.

She walked in and closed the door behind her. His wife Stacy was there. She was the local sports journalist, but she sometimes covered other news when they were short-staffed. With one journalist out from surgery and the other one out on maternity leave, everyone had to do their part and pitch in.

"Hi, Olivia." Stacy smiled.

"Hello yourself." Olivia's lips tipped up into a little smile. "I hear congratulations are in order."

"Yes, thank you. We're very excited." Stacy looked at Trent, who squeezed her hand and winked at her. She glanced back at Olivia and gave her a sympathetic look. "I'm so sorry this happened when you're not even settled yet. What a lousy welcome this has been. Nasty weather and now a dead body."

Olivia blew out a breath. "It comes with the territory, but I'm afraid this time it's worse than just a dead body."

Trent's lips turned down, and his eyebrows drew together. "How so?"

She inhaled a deep breath before dropping the bomb. "You have a homicide on your hands, Sheriff."

His eyes widened and he cursed under his breath before rubbing his forehead. "That's what I was afraid of."

Stacy gasped. "Are you sure?"

"Positive," Olivia continued. "The victim's lungs are clear. There's no water inside. That means she didn't drown. She was dead before entering the water."

"She?" Stacy's face paled.

"A female in her late twenties. Her body is fairly well-preserved from the ice and snow, but her fingerprints weren't intact enough for me to identify her. I'm using her dental records, but that can take a while. My last resort will be her DNA, which takes the longest to return results. My full report will determine more, but I wanted to let you know she was definitely murdered." Olivia handed Trent the report. "She died of blunt force trauma to the head. Her skull clearly shows that, but given the length of time since she died and her body lying in water for that long, it will be difficult to determine much else."

"Maybe it wasn't murder. Maybe she fell and hit her head, then rolled into the water." Hope filled Trent's voice.

Olivia was already shaking her head. "The injury isn't indicative of a fall, where her head would do the hitting. From what I can tell, an object was used to strike against her head, leaving a distinct impression imbedded in her skull."

"It was worth a shot. Thank you." Trent sighed gravely. "Keep me posted when you discover more."

"You can count on me."

"Okay, so it was murder. That we know for sure. But she could have been killed any number of places and washed into The Cove with the spring thaw," Stacy offered. "It doesn't necessarily mean she was murdered here, right?"

"That's a possibility," Olivia replied objectively. She'd been trained to push her emotions aside and focus on the facts.

"Let's hope that's the case." Trent looked at Stacy. "Do me a favor, hon, and keep this under wraps until we know what we're dealing with, okay?"

"I can try, but you know how it is in a small town. The rumor mill has most likely already spread the news across several counties."

"Still, no one knows she was murdered, and I'd like to keep it that way. Maine is a harsh place to live. Unfortunately, people die all the time around these parts, but murder is a whole other matter." He picked up his phone.

"Who are you calling?" Stacy asked.

"Laura." The lines between his eyes deepened. "It's time to start planning for damage control."

Olivia closed the door behind her as she headed back to the lab to run more tests and exhaust all her efforts. Why did it have to be blunt-force trauma to the head? She clenched her fists to stop her hands from shaking. Death was a part of her profession, but she'd left New York to get away from murder.

She wasn't at all sure she could handle another homicide.

* * *

"Wow, you weren't kidding when you said you would hook me up." Zoe sat at a table in The Claw in front of the windows, overlooking the harbor.

The orange-red ball of the sun sank lower in the sky, casting a fiery glow over the dark water. Sitting alone at a table for dinner didn't bother her. She was used to being on her own. Had been since she was eighteen and could leave the foster system.

Her mother had been a druggie and her father in prison, so the state had taken Zoe and her two brothers, Dan and Scott, when she was five, and split them up. Never having been adopted, she'd learned early on not to count on anyone but herself. Recently, they'd found each other again and were trying to reform bonds, but things were different now that so much time had passed. It was hard to feel like she even knew them anymore.

"Hey, people around here keep their promises. I owed you one." Jack set a heaping plate of New England boiled dinner in front of her, pulling her from her depressing thoughts.

"All I did was recommend your place. No biggie." She eyed him suspiciously, not used to all this attention from anyone, let alone an attractive man. She blinked. *Attractive?* Now where had that thought come from? She couldn't afford to lose focus ever again.

Bad things happened when she lost focus.

The aromas of flavorful turnips, onions, carrots,

beets, new potatoes, cabbage, garlic, and salty corned beef hit her senses, making her mouth water, and pulling her thoughts away from dangerous territory. He set a small loaf of warm Irish soda bread on a small plate to the side, with a cup of softened butter. She couldn't stop a little groan from slipping out of her mouth.

He grinned.

She frowned.

"Word-of-mouth means more than you know." His gaze traced over her pale wavy hair, face, and body. He snapped his gaze back to her wary one and cleared his throat. "Sorry, you uh, look much different out of your uniform."

"Thanks, I think." She tucked a strand of hair behind her ear, not liking the vulnerable feelings coursing through her.

She'd left her hair down after her shift and changed into a pair of jeans and a light-blue sweater that brought out the color of her eyes. That was the extent of getting dressed up for her. She'd always been a tomboy, never caring about makeup and dresses. Her hair style consisted of simple waves falling past her shoulders that she could pull back in a low bun for work.

Easy and efficient.

"You're welcome," he replied carefully. "It was definitely a compliment." His face looked pensive as if he were talking to himself. "I've never seen hair such a pale shade of blonde before. And your eyelashes are so long, not to mention your eyes are the color of clear-blue Caribbean water. Your whole look fascinates me."

"Are you always so blunt?" She stared at him, drawing her eyebrows together and tilting her lips down.

"No." He shook his head, looking baffled. "Sorry

again. Obviously, my brain is behind my mouth. I simply meant you have a very unique look."

She'd take *unique*. It was better than the comments she usually got. "It's fine. You're not the first to talk about my looks." She shrugged. "That's why I like my uniform so much. I can hide beneath my hat."

"*Unique* is a good thing, Zoe," Jack's voice softened. "Trust me when I say you have nothing to hide."

Her eyes met his, and she felt her cheeks fill with heat. He'd called her by her first name. She swallowed hard, unable to speak. That was a first for her.

"Enjoy your dinner." He tipped his head and then made his way back behind the bar, his *The Claw* t-shirt hugging his muscles.

And damned if she didn't watch his every step.

Well, hell.

* * *

LAURA SAT around the large table in the conference room of the town hall. David Garcia and his assistants, Hannah Simpson and Jude Lawrence, joined her to discuss the upcoming spring festival season.

"So, what would you like to start with?" David folded his hands on the table in front of him.

He had olive skin and tight, black curly hair. What he lacked in height, he made up for in appearance. He was always fashionably dressed in designer clothes, sporting fancy shoes and a watch that cost as much as her car, Laura thought. His services were expensive, but he came highly recommended by several other mayors up and down the coast for the effect his events had on their towns. Still, she felt uneasy about spending so much money. The town couldn't afford for this effort to fail, but David Garcia was the best.

Right now, that was exactly what Coldwater Cove needed.

She looked down at her notes in front of her and then back up at him. "Don't you need a notebook and pen to write this down?"

"I have a photographic memory. I never forget an image." He held out his hand. "May I see that?" She handed over the paper, and he scanned the sheet for a minute and then handed it back to her. "You may continue whenever you're ready."

"Okay, then." She looked back at her paper, hoping she'd made the right decision. "I want to start with Maple Sunday. It's the third week in March and tradition around these parts. Then we can move into Spring Fest, followed by Moose Mania, and end with the Food, Wine, and Art Festival. That's always our biggest attraction, and I asked the museum to order some wonderful new pieces of art for the auction."

"Good to know." David opened the calendar on his phone. "Your plan sounds great, but we'll have to get started right away if we're going to be ready for Maple Sunday in time." He looked at the woman beside him. "Hannah, draw up a plan and get it to me for approval as soon as possible, please."

"Of course." She pushed her chic glasses up her nose, tucking her slicked-back, light-brown hair behind her ears before jotting something down in her notebook.

"Thank you. You're the best." David winked at her.

A little smile crossed her face, and she nodded once.

David looked at the man beside her. "Once Hannah's plan is approved, draw up a financial estimate for the mayor, Jude. We need to get the town's approval so we can move on to contacting our vendors."

Jude was a walking Ken doll, complete with sandy-blond hair that was parted on the side and a powder-blue suit. He looked up from his paper long enough to acknowledge David. "Right away, Boss." Then went back to making his own notes.

A knock sounded on Laura's door before Olivia walked in and stopped short. "Oh, I'm terribly sorry. I didn't realize you were in a meeting. That's no excuse for walking in without being invited. I should have made an appointment." She held up a folder she carried and looked at Laura. "I've had a development in the murder case and wanted to update you, but I can come back later."

"We're pretty much finished here, so no worries, Ms…?" David stood and walked over to Olivia, holding out his hand.

"Dr. Jones." She shook his hand, her gaze not quite meeting his, and she didn't ask who he was, either.

Olivia was a peculiar woman, Laura thought, wondering what her deal was. Either way, she was a genius they couldn't afford to lose.

"It's nice to meet you, Dr. Jones. I'm David Garcia of Garcia Events, and these are my assistants, Hannah Simpson and Jude Lawrence. If you give us five minutes to finish up, the mayor's all yours." His eyes never left Olivia's face. "And if you have some free time later, I would love to get to know you better."

Olivia was a beautiful woman who happened to be shorter than he. That had to be appealing to a man like David. Judging by the look in his eyes, he was fascinated with her. Laura looked at Olivia with curiosity.

The feeling did *not* appear to be mutual.

"I-um-I'm really busy, but maybe some other time, Mr. Garcia." Olivia turned to face Laura. "I'll be out in the hall when you're finished."

Laura nodded and watched Olivia quickly close the door behind her, with David still staring intensely in the direction she had left.

Laura cleared her throat. "I hate to be a downer, but do you think the murder investigation will keep people away from the festivals?"

Her stomach tightened into knots. News of the murder had spread faster than gale-force winds, just as she had feared it would. She could only hope that when they identified the woman who had been murdered, she wouldn't be from The Cove or a tourist who had been murdered in the cove. If the murder happened someplace else, then locals and tourists wouldn't be afraid to come to town and partake in the festivals.

David looked at Hannah and Jude for a moment and then shrugged as he turned his attention back on Laura. "I don't think the murder will affect anything. I heard the woman who was discovered has been dead for a while now. Anything could have happened to her anywhere. People up and down the coast know all sorts of things wash ashore during the spring thaw. It's come to be expected."

"In our line of work, you would be amazed at what we've seen," Jude added, a sympathetic expression crossing his face.

"I've never understood it, but for some reason, a lot of people have a morbid curiosity over that sort of thing." Hannah shivered. "It's sad to say, but if anything, it might draw even bigger crowds."

Laura's stomach turned over. She didn't think the woman who had been killed was anyone she knew from The Cove, because she couldn't think of anyone she hadn't seen around lately. Any murder was horrible, but losing one of their own would be awful. The Cove was existing in a terrible reality right now. "At least there's one small, positive effect of such a horrible tragedy. Bigger crowds mean more money spent in town. After the damage from the storm, we need all the money we can get, plain and simple."

"Then you need us," David said, in a matter-of-fact way. "We *can* help you, Laura, and we will. You just have to trust us to do our jobs and give us free rein. Deal?" He held out his hand.

Being the mayor, giving free rein to anyone was hard for her to do. She liked being in control, but with everything riding on these festivals, she had no other choice. She took a big breath and nodded as she shook his hand. "Deal."

He'd better be worth every cent.

3

Sheriff Trent West sat in his office, poring over his notes. So far, they had nothing, and his investigation was running cold. He needed a Hail Mary, big time.

"The dental record report came in." Oliva held another folder in her hand as she entered his office. "I already updated the mayor this morning when you were out of your office. Now that you're back, I'd like to fill you in as well."

"By all means." Trent was ready for any news that might help.

"Bodies that are missing for more than thirty days use dental records to identify the corpse once it's found," she continued as if she was unsure if a small-town sheriff would know these things.

He was already nodding. "I used to be part of the FBI before becoming Sheriff. I know all about the National Dental Image/Information Repository or NDIR. The FBI's Criminal Justice Information System known as CJIS created NDIR in 2005 to help identify missing, unidentified, and wanted persons."

Her eyes sprang wide. "You left the FBI to become a small-town sheriff?" She blinked. "Sorry, you don't have to answer that. It's none of my business." She masked her expressions, clearly not wanting him to pry into her personal life in return.

There was a time not long ago when he felt the same way. "I don't mind. It was time for me to move on, and a crazy redhead might have had something to do with it." His lips twitched in amusement, thinking of his wife and how much he adored her. "Anyway, the NDIR is a great tool for all law enforcement agencies."

"Agreed. Teeth are surprisingly durable. I took x-rays in the lab and submitted them to the database. We have a match." Her gray eyes remained objective and expressionless, which was needed for the job, but it made it difficult to read her.

Trent couldn't quite figure Olivia Jones out. She'd left a prestigious job in a big city to travel to the north-ernmost part of Maine, in small town Coldwater Cove. They couldn't afford to pay her what she was worth, but she didn't seem to care. She said she'd had enough of city life and was ready for a small town. He couldn't find anything on her before five years ago, but he didn't press the issue. Her references were impeccable.

And he was desperate for help, especially now.

"Please tell me she's not from these parts." Trent held his breath.

"Her name is Penelope Kensington. She's twenty-nine and from Connecticut. A wealthy socialite. She went missing right before the city got hit with winter storms. I think she floated north, got trapped in a frozen inlet somewhere, and eventually washed ashore with the spring thaw. I've notified her parents. They'll be here tomorrow, in case there's anything else you need for your investigation before I release her body."

"I'm relieved it's not one of our own, but her poor parents. She was so young." He scrubbed a hand over his whiskered jaw. "Thank you for letting me know. I'll definitely want to question her parents about anything she might have been into and any possible enemies she might have had."

Olivia nodded. "If there's nothing else, I'm going to work on finalizing the autopsy report."

"That's all for now."

She started to leave.

"One more thing, Olivia?"

She turned around with raised brows.

"I used to be just like you. All about the job." Shutting people out and carrying around a few demons of his own had been his sole existence, until a light had come into his life and lifted him up. "Try to take some time for yourself before you burn out." An empathetic smile swept over his face. "My wife taught me that."

Olivia's face flushed pink, and she nodded once, then quickly left his office.

Well, that was at least *some* reaction out of her. And that was a start.

* * *

ONE WEEK LATER, Olivia found herself attending the first festival of the spring season. Maple Sunday involved hopping from maple house to maple house, seeing demonstrations of how they tap the sap, then taking tours of the sugarhouses with further demonstrations on how maple syrup is made from boiled sap.

She found a new appreciation for maple syrup after learning it took forty liters of sap to make one liter of maple syrup, when most maple trees only yield between five and fifteen gallons of sap per season.

Oliva had learned about the taste, colors, and different grades of syrup, and then sampled an endless supply of maple desserts. She ate ice cream, donuts, fudge, and muffins after already indulging in maple-sausage fennel pizza, paired with a decadent maple stout. Her stomach was ready to burst, but she didn't regret her decision to get out of the lab.

Trent had questioned the victim's parents without much luck. The victim had a few charities and hobbies she was into, same as most of the people who ran in her social circle, as well as a tumultuous on-again-off-again relationship with a boyfriend who had an alibi. With no other reason to detain them further, he'd had to let them go. They had claimed Penelope's body and headed back to Connecticut.

Trent continued his investigation, and Olivia went back to organizing Clive's Catastrophe and cleaning up her lab. She'd thought about what Trent had said to her. That she needed a better work life balance. So, when Stacy asked Zoe and her to go to the festival to support Laura and the town, Olivia had forced herself to say yes.

She had gone to therapy and had been in a good place for a while... until the recent incident that had made her nightmares come back. Her mother had always told her if something isn't working for you, then change it up. That was why she'd moved to Coldwater Cove. To change things up.

That started with saying *yes* more often.

"I can't eat another bite." Zoe groaned.

She'd gone with a sporty casual vibe, looking pretty in jeans and a sweatshirt with her pale blonde hair down loose. Softer. Less tough. Olivia couldn't help but wonder if a certain pub owner had anything to do with it. From what she'd witnessed, there were definite sparks snapping between them.

"Me either, and I'm eating for two." Stacy rubbed her barely-rounded, red-flannel-covered stomach that made her wild hair stand out even more. She'd worn leggings and rubber rain boots, looking cozy yet stylish. "How about you, Olivia? Are you doing okay?"

"I'm fine, thank you." Olivia smoothed a hand down her sweater and slacks, her long hair in her standard braid. Routine and familiarity comforted her, she thought, as she wrapped her hand around her cross. She wasn't really fine, but she would be. She was determined to be. That was why she was here.

She would never progress if she didn't step outside of her comfort zone.

"Good, then let's go to the community center." Stacy beamed excitedly. "There is a maple exhibit with antiques and crafts. Laura said there will be fun contests and a youth talent show. Then out front on Main Street there will be a sap run road race, followed by a parade and evening entertainment."

"Don't forget about the horse-drawn sleigh rides, wagon rides, cooking demonstrations, and sugar-on-snow parties." Zoe chuckled. Even though it was spring, there was still some patchy snow on the ground. "Garcia Events went all out on planning this first festival. Hopefully, it pays off."

"It had better, for what David charged Laura," Stacy muttered.

A few minutes later, they arrived at the community center. They'd ridden in Stacy's new SUV that Trent had insisted she buy for their growing family. Olivia didn't mind. Even though she'd lived in New York for the past five years, she still didn't like driving in the snow. Not after growing up in the south.

After parking the car, they went inside. Laura and her husband Tommy—who towered above her—walked over to them with the cutest blonde-haired twin girls. They had their mother's looks, but their father's height for sure.

"Hey, Tommy." Stacy waved.

Tommy nodded, his hands full with holding his daughters.

Then Stacy hugged Laura hard. "This looks fantastic!"

"You think so?" Laura pulled back and scanned the room with a critical eye.

"Absolutely," Zoe chimed in. "Garcia has outdone himself."

Olivia glanced over to where David, Hannah, and Jude stood in different sections of the community center with mics on, radioing each other to keep things on track. Meanwhile, Larry was on a ladder, fixing a leak in the roof in the back. Most of the town was in attendance.

Olivia followed Zoe's gaze across the room. Jack and his parents were talking to the Sheriff.

"I'll catch up with you ladies later," Zoe said. "I have to talk to Trent about something." She made a beeline for the group before any of them had a chance to say a word.

"Someone's got a crush." Stacy's eyes followed Zoe.

"Sure looks that way," Laura added.

Olivia watched Zoe briefly stop to talk to the Sheriff, then focus her attention on Jack and his parents. "He seems like a nice guy."

"Jack is about as genuine as they come." Stacy studied him as she talked. "He's been through a lot. So has Zoe."

"Haven't we all." Laura let out a scoff and shook her head. "But I'm rooting for them. They deserve to be happy." She looked at Olivia. "How about you, Olivia? Is there anyone special in your life?"

Olivia's stomach flipped. She hated talking about herself. "Let's just say I've been through a lot, too." She clasped her hands together to keep from fidgeting. "I'm not very good with people. At least the ones that are alive, anyway."

They all laughed.

"You just haven't met the right *living* person." Stacy reached out and squeezed her hand. "You're doing just fine with people, from what I've seen. Maybe Coldwater Cove will turn things around for you. It has a way of doing that for people. Trent and me. Jack's sister Emma and her boyfriend Gunner. Her friends Harvey and JoJo. Now, hopefully, Jack and Zoe, and then maybe you."

"Maybe." Olivia smiled a little.

She had always wanted to fall in love and have a family. But after her parents died in a car crash when she was in college, her medical degree had become her focus. Then later, when she finished her residency and the unthinkable had happened, she'd moved to New York with one sole purpose. Blending in. Disappearing.

Surviving.

Now, after five years of just getting by, she was done with surviving. She wanted to start thriving. Her parents would have wanted that for her, and she owed it to them not to waste the rest of her life. She'd told herself to be open to new possibilities. She needed to keep reminding herself of that every time she got scared.

Raised voices drew the attention of everyone in the room.

"Who are they?" Olivia asked.

"That would be Miley Hart, Bryce Ferrone, and Derks Callaway," Stacy replied with a frown as she watched them. "They are Coldwater Cove's Little League coaches."

"Who is the poor woman they're yelling at?" Olivia studied the pretty brunette. Her face was flushed as she took a step back from the trio, looking uncomfortable.

"That would be Fay Allenby," Laura chimed in with a disapproving tone. "She's the museum director, and I can guess what this is about." Laura sighed and rubbed her temples. "Duty calls." Tommy took the girls away towards the kids' corner of crafts, while Laura marched over to the group with Stacy and Olivia hot on her heels.

David Garcia got to Fay first, putting himself between her and the coaches.

"Break it up, people. Nothing to see here." Trent shooed several onlookers away as he faced the trio. "Care to explain?"

"Yeah, I'll gladly explain. I saw the shipment that arrived this morning. That was quite a haul." Bryce placed his hands on his hips. "Why is expensive new art for the museum more important than new uniforms for our team?"

"That new art will be auctioned off during the Food, Wine, and Art Festival," Garcia interjected. "The potential profit can't be denied."

"And a good chunk of that will line your pockets, I'm sure," Bryce growled.

Laura stood straighter and folded her hands in front of her. "As mayor, one of the most important parts of my job is to bring in new money for the town."

Derks stepped forward. "As head coach, I can tell you we're on track for making it to the Little League World Series. That will bring more people to town for sure."

"I understand what you're saying, Mr. Calloway, but we need money right now." Laura kept her voice calm and diplomatic. "Once The Cove is back on its feet, we will make sure your team has uniforms for next year."

"Next year will be too late," Miley jumped in. "Little League players range from nine to twelve years old. We have a star pitcher. A girl who is twelve, so this is her last year. She deserves to look as good as she plays while she's still a part of the team. If we make it to the World Series, this girl will make the national news."

"Sports are unpredictable," Stacy added in her objective journalist tone. "The Cove needs a sure thing after all it has been through. No matter how good your team is, you can't be certain you will win."

"I don't know why they insist on taking things out on me." Fay's voice hitched, and David patted her shoulder. "I'm just doing my job. Besides, the arts are just as important as sports."

"That's an age-old conflict that will never be solved." Trent looked at all of them. "This isn't the time or place for causing a scene."

"And this isn't over," Derks ground out. "You can be sure of that." He, Miley, and Bryce turned around and stormed out of the community center, leaving an unsettling current weaving through the air.

* * *

THE NEXT MORNING, Olivia went to The Lost Horizon for breakfast before work. The Lost Horizon was a diner, sporting pictures of The Cove in all its glorious seasons. Under new ownership by a local woman, Betty Clark, the menu was filled with classic homecooked meals that reminded Olivia of her mother's cooking.

The bell over the door chimed, and in walked realtors Tia, Calvin, and Dijon Johnson. Tia spotted Olivia and said something to her brothers, who glanced over at her. Calvin waved and kept walking, while Dijon stared a moment longer than was comfortable before nodding and following his brother to the hostess station.—

Tia headed Olivia's way.

Olivia felt a blush creep up her neck.

"Hi, Olivia." Tia smiled wide. "Don't mind my brothers. I think Dijon has a little crush on you."

"Really? He's never spoken to me." Olivia studied the handsome man, but looked away the second they made eye contact. "I'm not really in a good place for a relationship, especially now with all the work I have to do."

"He's harmless." Tia changed the subject. "Enough about my brothers. Tell me, how are you settling in?"

"I'm managing just fine." Olivia sipped her coffee. "I didn't have much to unpack because I don't have many possessions."

"Well, you would be one of a few who could say that." Tia put her hand on the chair across from Olivia. "May I sit?"

"Sure." Olivia nodded, finishing the last bite of her sausage-and-egg casserole and picking up her coffee mug once more, cradling it to warm her hands. "What can I help you with?"

"I'm just checking in to see how you're doing. I know it hasn't been easy with a murder happening so soon after you got here, but that just means we need you more than ever. I hope we didn't scare you away."

"I don't have any plans to move as of yet. I love my job. Always have. It's just finding the perfect fit of a place that I'm looking for to settle down permanently."

"Oh, good, I'm so happy you like it here." Tia's glance shot over to her brothers, who were still watching them. She sat up a little straighter and narrowed her eyes. "It's hard being the youngest Johnson. I feel like I have to prove myself to my family all the time."

"Families can be difficult, but cherish the fact that you still have one," Olivia said softly, failing at hiding her emotions when it came to discussing her family.

Tia's gaze snapped to hers and widened. "I am so sorry. I can't believe I said that out loud. That wasn't very professional of me."

"It's okay. Sometimes it's easier to talk to an outsider." Olivia's lips tipped up a little. She liked Tia.

Tia relaxed slightly. "Forget the sales pitch, and let's start over. I genuinely am happy you are here. I'm new to town, too, and don't have many friends yet."

"Well, you have one in me."

"You have no idea how thankful I am to hear that." Tia stood. "Maybe we can get together sometime and go out for a drink."

Olivia took a deep breath. "Yes." She exhaled, realizing her feelings of anxiety were lessening.

Tia beamed, looking genuinely pleased. "Great. I'll be in touch."

"I look forward to it."

Olivia watched Tia walk back to her brothers, her steps lighter and her posture not so rigid. It felt good making a new friend, and saying *yes* hadn't been as difficult as she'd thought it would be. Maybe things were finally starting to turn around for her.

She flagged down the waitress for her bill when her cell phone rang.

"Dr. Jones here."

"Can you meet me at the museum?" Sheriff West asked.

"I was just about to head back to my office and tackle more file boxes." She noted a weariness in the Sheriff's voice as if he'd pulled an all-nighter. "Is everything all right?"

A long pause filled the line before the Sheriff finally spoke.

"We have another dead body."

4

OLIVIA ARRIVED at the museum to a swarm of law enforcement officers, crime scene investigators, and emergency responders, as well as half the town standing back behind police tape. The Sheriff stood out front talking to the mayor, and they both wore grave expressions.

That was not promising.

A body from out of town washing ashore during the spring thaw was difficult enough to handle. But a murder being committed right in The Cove during a much-needed festival season was a public relations nightmare.

"Sheriff. Mayor." Olivia nodded as she reached them.

Trent looked around at the growing crowd and then at Laura, before meeting Olivia's gaze. "Follow me."

They all went inside and headed towards Stacy in the lobby. She was talking to Nolan Turner, the Assistant Museum Director, who looked visibly upset. Olivia came to a jarring stop, sucking in a sharp breath. This was worse than just a murder being committed in town.

The victim was one of their own.

Fay Allenby, the museum director, lay flat on her back on the floor by the front desk in a pool of blood. Olivia took a moment to compose herself and then bent down to conduct an initial assessment. Fay's head was bashed in, just like Penelope's…

Just like before.

Olivia moved the edge of Fay's blouse to the side and looked at the skin just beneath her collarbone. Her heart started to pound, and she let go of the shirt. Her body shielded anyone from seeing what she just saw. She needed to examine the rest of her body in private to be sure. Breathing slowly, she counted to ten before moving away to stand up and meet the Sheriff's questioning eyes.

"When your crew is finished, have the body taken to the crime lab. I'll get started right away."

"You got it."

"I don't understand any of this. Who would do such a thing?" Laura asked. "Fay was a good person. A friend. What on earth is going on around here?"

"I'll see if anything was taken. Maybe it was just a robbery. Maybe there isn't any connection between Fay and Penelope." Trent made a note in a small notebook he carried and gave Zoe instructions.

"Well, they both had their skulls bashed in." Laura folded her arms around herself and shivered. "I'd say that's pretty similar." She pressed her trembling lips together for a moment. "I'll tell Fay's family. I know she didn't live here for long, but I knew her better than anyone else in town."

Olivia and Trent nodded their consent.

"I feel horrible. Maple Sunday was a success. David wants to use the momentum for Spring Fest next week and Moose Mania after that. All our efforts are building towards the Food, Wine, and Art Festival as the grand finale. Fay was supposed to be a big part of that. It won't be the same without her."

"It will be okay, Laura." Stacy hugged her. "I can't buy you time with this story. There are too many people outside who have heard what happened, and then there's the media, who are already showing up from other towns. I have a colleague I'm going to call to see if he will help us. But rest assured, Trent and I will get to the bottom of this. We'll find out what happened to Fay. I can promise you that."

"And I will focus solely on this murder." Olivia kept her suspicions to herself for now. "I'll have my report back to Trent as soon as possible."

Penelope's body had been too decomposed to see if she had any more similarities with Fay other than the blunt force trauma to the head. Further examination would reveal if Olivia's suspicions were true. And if they were, then her nightmares weren't over with yet.

What Olivia had just seen on Fay... she had seen before.

* * *

SPECIAL AGENT HANK MASTERS sat in Coldwater Cove's sheriff's office, waiting for the Sheriff to arrive. He looked over the report before him for the tenth time, yet he was still in disbelief. He worked out of the FBI field office in Boston, Massachusetts, which covered the state of Maine. Sometimes the FBI clashed with other law enforcement agencies on jurisdiction, but lucky for him, Sheriff Trent West was a former special agent.

West had actually reached out to Hank's office, asking for a profiler, saying the matter was urgent. Hank had volunteered to go. When Trent had faxed the autopsy reports over, the contents had shocked Hank.

Two victims. Blunt force trauma to the head. Branded with the letter D.

His body hummed with adrenaline over the third fact. It was only one body. The other had been too decomposed for him to be sure she had been branded as well, but it was a start. Five years ago, the case he had been working on went cold. That had haunted him for reasons he'd buried. He'd never forgotten or gotten over not being able to put the bastard away, and had spent every day since still searching for leads.

This was the first substantial lead he'd had in years.

A man walked through the door and held out his hand. "Special Agent Masters, it's good to meet you. Sorry I'm late."

Hank shook his hand. "Glad to be of help, Sheriff West, and no worries. I'm actually a little early."

"That's completely fine. Now that the story is all over the news, we could use all the help we can get. Follow me. There's someone I want you to meet."

Hank stood and followed the Sheriff down the hall to the crime lab. A petite woman with a long, dark braid hanging over a white lab coat stood working with her back to them.

Trent stopped right behind her. "Special Agent Masters, I'd like you to meet our medical examiner, Dr. Jones."

The woman jumped a little before turning around. "Sheriff, you scared me." She held a hand over her chest.

"Sorry about that." Trent tilted his head and then stepped out of the way.

Hank felt like he'd been sucker-punched to the gut as he stared at eyes full of gray storm clouds. She couldn't be over five feet tall, carrying a petite frame. He had to pull from all the skills he'd learned over his years as an FBI agent to school his features and not show the effect she had on him.

Standing over a foot taller than her, he held out his hand. "It's good to meet you, Dr. Jones. You can call me Hank." He tried for a smile but couldn't manage one, knowing his face must look so serious. Then again, the situation called for serious.

She eyed him a little warily as she shook his hand. "I'm Olivia."

Giving up on pleasantries, he focused on the facts. "I read your report." He held up the folder in his other hand. "I've seen this before. Branded with the letter D just below the collarbone."

She was already shaking her head *no*, seeming more comfortable with sticking to the facts as well. "I know what you're thinking. We might have a serial killer on our hands, but I don't think so."

Hank frowned. "What makes you say that?"

Her gaze locked with his. "I know the case you're talking about."

The Sheriff eyed her curiously. "Really?"

Her face flushed just a tiny bit, but Hank had been trained to look for even the faintest of a reaction. His gaze met Trent's, and they both continued to study her in silence.

"I mean, I can't imagine anyone who doesn't know that case. It was all over the news back then." She raised her chin a notch. "The Cattleman Killer."

"That's right." Hank remembered the first time he'd heard about it. He'd been hanging out with his brother and sister at a bar and saw the news come on, having no idea the impact the case would have on their lives. He cleared his throat. "Miami five years ago. The killer branded his victims with the letter D just below their collarbone, raped them, and then bashed their skulls in.

Five successful women with dark hair, in their late twenties, died, except for one."

"The one that got away." Trent wrinkled his forehead. "I remember that case now."

Hank nodded slowly. "She was lucky enough to survive, although, I wouldn't exactly call her lucky. She had to have gone through unspeakable acts." His face pinched, and he forced himself to block out the painful memories trying to break free. "A woman by the name of Lilly Swanson, but she disappeared. The killer got away and hasn't emerged since."

Trent's gaze followed Hank's, to study Olivia intensely.

Hank replied, "Until now."

She stood a little straighter, her face devoid of all emotion as she spoke in an objective, businesslike tone. "*Not* now. Initially, I thought maybe the real killer was back. Penelope died by blunt force trauma to the head, but her body was so decomposed, there is no way to tell if she had been branded or raped. As for Fay, she was branded and died by blunt force trauma to her head as well, but she wasn't raped. The MO is a little different."

"You both thinking what I'm thinking?" Trent removed his hat to run a hand over his buzz cut before returning it.

"I think we have a copycat on our hands," Olivia responded.

"Someone wants us to think The Cattleman Killer has come out from hiding." Hank rubbed his whiskered jaw, realizing he needed a shave. He'd dropped everything when the Sheriff had called him, packing a bag, and driving up the coast right away. He hadn't even checked into his hotel yet.

"Whoever the copycat is, they don't want us to know the real reason for the murder." Trent frowned.

"But why choose The Cattleman Killer? This isn't Florida. What could possibly be so appealing about a small town in northern Maine?"

"The woman who got away." Hank kept his eyes on the Sheriff. "Whatever crime is really going on will be buried beneath the media The Cattleman Killer will draw. It's one hell of a good cover."

"What are you saying, Masters?" Trent asked.

"Why don't you ask Dr. Jones?" Hank's gaze slid back to Olivia's.

Her eyes widened a fraction, but she didn't waver or look away. He was impressed by how brave she was being and couldn't help softening toward her. There was something about her that made him want to wrap her in his arms and tell her everything would be okay. But he wasn't here for that. He was here to do his job, no matter the cost this time.

"Is there something that you two know that I don't?" Trent looked back and forth between them.

Olivia sighed, letting go of the cross pendant on her necklace. "Yes, Sheriff." She looked him in the eyes, standing as straight and tall as she could. "Olivia was my mother's middle name and Jones was my father's middle name. My name used to be Lilly Swanson, but I buried her five years ago and moved to New York City to start over."

Trent gaped and took a moment to shake off his stupor. "I thought you looked familiar, but your hair is a lot longer now," he mused, still looking a little dazed. "I'm so sorry for all you've been through. You're very brave."

"Not really. Changing my identity didn't stop the nightmares every time a new murder happened. Therapy helped me overcome a lot. Life wasn't so bad anymore. I was even happy for a while. Normal. Until I had to testify in a recent murder case."

"In your line of work, I would think you would be used to testifying in court cases." Hank studied her carefully.

"I am. Until the perpetrator in that case got loose and attacked me, right on the stand. It took several people to pull him off me, and well, that set me back years, right back to square one." She inhaled a shaky breath. "So, I decided I'd had enough of big cities and moved north to a small town, hoping I could finally find peace. We see how well that turned out."

Hank muttered a curse under his breath, anger filling him for what this courageous woman had gone through. "I'm surprised you didn't quit after that."

"I thought about it, but I truly love the science of what I do, and the answers and peace it brings to loved ones." She shook her head. "I just don't understand how someone found me here in such a small, remote town."

"Your name might be different, and your hair longer and braided, but your face and eyes are unforgettable," Hank said softly, then cleared his throat. "Someone must have recognized you, is all I'm saying."

"There are a lot of new people in town, and it *is* the tourist season. It could be anyone," Trent speculated. "Do you think you could recognize the killer if you saw him?"

"No. He wore a ski mask. He covered my head with a burlap bag and took me deep into the woods." She plucked at the hem of her lab coat, pausing a beat. "A man was the killer, but he had help. I think there were three of them. I kept hearing another man and a woman, but he only ever talked to them outside. He never let them see or speak to me, like he was a control freak. I was his alone. He was the only one to ever come into the room where they kept me. I will never forget *his* voice. It was laced with pure evil and filled with a bone-chilling hatred."

"What are you going to do?" Trent asked.

"I'm not running anymore." She ran her hand down the length of her braid all the way to her small waist, looking vulnerable. "I just can't."

"You don't have to." Trent rested his hand on his holster. "You're not alone. You have me, for one."

"And I'm not going anywhere." Hank clenched his fists to keep from hugging her. He couldn't do anything before, but he damn sure could now.

Olivia nodded. "Thank you both for that. What happens next?"

"We find out who this copycat killer is, and what exactly he's up to." Trent headed for the door. "I have some calls to make."

"And we have a conversation we need to have." Hank looked Olivia in the eye, wishing he could tell her everything, but it was too risky right now. "Do you trust me?"

"Do I have a choice?"

The silence was deafening.

* * *

SHERIFF WEST and Mayor Flemming stood in front of a podium, holding their press conference. Rows of chairs filled the room, with standing-room-only left in the back. The whole town was present, along with all sorts of media and tourists crowding together, buzzing with their concerns, their *fears*.

Not me. I stood off to the side, out of the way, listening and observing.

Always watching.

My gaze swept the room, settling on the petite woman standing on the opposite side of the room.

Fury burned like acid in my gut and the breath in my chest quickened. Whatever they were saying turned to garbled sound waves in my head, until she moved to stand by their side at the podium.

They introduced her as Medical Examiner Dr. Olivia Jones, and she addressed the crowd looking high and mighty, like she thought she was better than everyone else. They always thought they were better than everyone else. Only, Dr. Olivia Jones wasn't fooling me. I knew exactly who she was the moment I saw her.

Lilly Swanson. The one fucking bitch who got away.

I'd agreed to stop the killings until we found the little slut and finished her off, never imagining it would take five fucking years. When I saw the news about The Cattleman Killer possibly emerging from hiding, I was livid. Copycats were wannabes. Get your own fucking MO. The branding was mine, dammit.

When I found out who dared *try* to copy me, I would torture them slowly after I thanked them for bringing me to *her*.

"You're getting angry," he whispered for my ears only. "People are going to see."

"Shut up," I hissed through my teeth, my eyes trained on the beautiful brunette, my second chance for victory dangling like a carrot before me. Being close to her again soothed some of my anger into annoyance. I needed to close our chapter before I could move on. I lowered my voice and responded, "No one else is over here except the three of us. I'm through listening to you."

"I agree with him," she added just as quietly. "We both understand what you've been through, but this isn't just about you. You can't risk everything we've worked for."

"I can do whatever the hell I want. I'm in charge now." I drew my eyes away from my gorgeous prey and tried not to glare as I kept my voice low and deadly.

"You'll do what I say, or I'll be done with both of you… for good." My accomplices could be a pain in the ass.

"You need us," she said calmly, always the voice of reason.

I fucking hated that about her.

"I'll find out what I can and figure out a way for us all to get what we want. You just have to be patient until we construct the perfect plan," he said, the brains of our operation.

I knew they were right. I couldn't accomplish my mission without either of them. I ground my teeth and forced myself to calm down. "I can be patient a little while longer, but that doesn't mean I can't have fun while I wait for the right time to finish what I started. I won't stop until I get what I want."

Buckle up, Olivia Jones. I'm coming for you, and I'm more than ready to play doctor.

5

OLIVIA POURED herself a glass of red wine and stepped out onto the patio of her cottage on the water. She was exhausted. Wrapping a blanket around herself, she sat in a wicker chair and turned on the propane fire pit. The days were getting warmer and growing longer, but the mid-spring evenings were still cool.

Taking a sip of wine, she sat in silence, staring out over the waves.

The sun was setting, casting orange, pink, and purple rays over the ocean, reflecting its image onto the surface. Images of Special Agent Hank Masters swam before her mind's eye. She'd never seen a more handsome man. He had neatly styled golden-blond hair, and deep-blue eyes that had burned into her, unsettling her to the core. She had guessed right away by the way that he looked at her that he had recognized her, but she had hoped she was wrong.

She wasn't.

So, she'd had no choice but to come clean. She had filled in Hank and the Sheriff the best she could on what had happened to her five years ago. She had been kidnapped, branded, and raped. The killer had put a burlap bag over her head when he took her to the woods so she wouldn't remember the way. Then he took the bag off so she would have to watch what he did to her. He tied her up in the woods in an abandoned shack where he'd left her for days, coming and going and inflicting his pain on her. She'd shouted out, hoping his accomplices would help her.

No one ever did.

He'd starved her, giving her only a small amount of water. Just enough to keep her alive. When he'd had his fill of her and figured she was too weak to fight back, he showed up with a tire iron. He didn't realize she'd worked at her bindings a little bit each day until she'd freed herself.

Being a doctor, she knew exactly how to incapacitate him. Catching him by surprise when she lunged at him, she'd wrestled the tire iron away from him and aimed for his knees, groin, and throat. When he fell, gasping for air, she'd run for all she was worth. Naked, afraid, alone, and in shock in the Florida woods, she'd finally found a road. Someone had pity on her and had stopped, wrapping her in a blanket and taking her to the hospital.

She'd told the police where the killer and his accomplices had kept her, but when the police got there, they were all gone.

Terrified he was still out there after her, she'd changed her name, packed just enough belongings to get by, and then fled. She hadn't cut her hair in five years. Using her inheritance from her parents, she settled in New York City and started over.

When you had money, it wasn't difficult to find shady people willing to forge documents. Olivia was fine with that because she wasn't stealing anyone's identity. She was the one who had gone to medical school, and the names she had chosen were her parents' middle names. She'd bought a special cross pendant and had her parents' names engraved on each side, hanging it on a long chain around her neck.

She hadn't taken it off since that day.

Trent and Hank had both agreed to keep her secret safe and help her get to the bottom of who the copycat was. Once they put the copycat away, she could go on with her life. For all she knew, the real killer wasn't even around anymore. And if he was, he lived in Florida.

A world away.

She trusted Trent completely. She wanted to trust Hank, but there was something he was hiding from her. She could feel it in her gut, yet her gut also said he was a good guy. She'd survived this long by following her gut, so that's what she intended to do.

The April showers had finally let up. The trees were full of buds, and birds had begun to fly back home for the warmer weather. She tightened her blanket around her as a breeze picked up. Sipping more wine, she listened to the water lap against the shore.

A twig snapped.

She surged up ramrod straight, knocking her wine glass over. Glass shattered everywhere and deep red liquid pooled on the cement, staining it. It was Maine, with woods all around. It was probably just an animal, but her gut was telling her it was more. Olivia jumped to her feet and spun around, but she didn't see anything.

Then why couldn't she shake this feeling that something was wrong?

She ran back inside her cottage and locked the door. Twirling around in circles, over and over, she still didn't see anything. She felt like she was losing her mind.

Suddenly, the smell of a man's cologne filled her nose.

It was a distinct scent of earth and musk she had only ever smelled on one man. Crippling fear filled her. Had he been here, invading her personal space, touching her things. Nausea filled her stomach and acid burned the back of her throat, choking her. Her heart started pounding, and her vision blurred.

She screamed for all she was worth, over and over until she was hoarse.

Someone pounded on her front door, and she screamed again.

"Olivia, it's me, Tia. Are you okay?"

Intense relief surged through Olivia, making her body weak and unsteady. Letting out a sob, she ran to the door, looked through the peephole, and wilted. She unlocked the latch with shaking hands and let Tia inside then closed and locked the door behind her.

Tia took one look at Olivia and wrapped her arms around her. "Oh, honey, it's okay. I'm here now."

After sobbing hysterically for several moments, Olivia finally calmed down. She stepped out of Tia's embrace and blew her nose. "I'm sorry."

"Don't be sorry. Something obviously has you spooked." She studied Olivia, waiting patiently.

"Want some wine?" Olivia wiped her eyes with shaking hands. "I need a glass, or two, or three."

"Sure thing. Let me just text my brothers. We were showing the cottage next door to Remy Finkelstein. He's been staying at the hotel since he took over as harbormaster. You scared me to death when I heard you scream. Voices carry on the water. I took off running. They're probably wondering what happened to me. Calvin's pretty chill, but Dijon can be a little overprotective. He is the oldest, after all." She rolled her eyes. "I'll let them know I'm at your place and not to wait for me. I will Uber home."

"Or you could spend the night. I have a guest bedroom, and I really don't want to be alone." Olivia felt her lips tremble.

"Done." Tia sent the text.

Olivia headed for her kitchen. Pouring two glasses of red wine, she carried them to the living room, where they sat down on the overstuffed couch.

"Do you smell men's cologne?" Olivia looked at Tia, praying she smelled it, too. She didn't want to believe she was going crazy.

Tia sniffed deeply a couple of times then gave her a look of sympathy. "I'm sorry, no. Why do you ask?"

Olivia shrugged. "I thought I smelled it when I came inside. Must be I'm imagining things." She liked Tia a lot, but she wasn't ready to reveal who she was to anyone else besides Trent and Hank. She didn't know if she ever would be. Even Stacy and Zoe didn't know the truth.

"That was no ordinary scream. It was filled with raw terror." Tia took a big sip of wine. "I felt your fear clear to my soul. What on earth happened?"

"I was sitting outside, enjoying a glass of wine and a fire, when I heard a twig snap. It's silly, I know, but with two murders happening so close together and the thought of a serial killer on the loose, I guess I let my imagination run away with me." Olivia shook her head. "When I came inside, it felt like someone had been in here. And then I smelled a man's cologne and freaked out. That's all."

"I'd say that's enough." Tia stared at her with wide eyes. "I would have freaked out, too. Now I wish I didn't show you this cottage. I don't like the idea of you being out here alone. The cottage next door is empty and hasn't sold yet, unless Remy decides he wants it. Either way, it could be a while before you have a neighbor. Maybe you should move."

"I'll be okay." Olivia laughed, feeling foolish now.

"My mother used to say I have a vivid imagination." Her smile faded as she looked at her friend with gratitude. "Thank you for caring about me. I'm glad you're here tonight."

"Me, too. Now how about another glass of wine and a romantic comedy to take our minds off scary things?"

"Nothing has ever sounded better."

"Great! Do you have anything I can borrow to sleep in? Anything that will fit, anyway." Tia eyed her doubtfully.

Tia was tall and curvy while Olivia was short and thin. But Olivia had kept some of her parents' clothes.

"You pick out the movie. I'll be right back." Olivia grabbed one of her father's t-shirts and an extra towel set then put them in her guest bedroom. She tried to brush off what had happened as a figment of her imagination, but the whisper from her gut was real.

The question was, would she listen to it this time.

* * *

THE NEXT DAY Olivia walked through the front door to The Claw and scanned the pub. Spotting Stacy at a table by the front windows, she headed in that direction to join her group. Trent had called a meeting, killing two birds with one stone since it was dinner time. The Claw was his favorite restaurant.

The place was packed with all the tourists in town for Spring Fest, and various journalists, from news stations to tabloids. Olivia stopped walking, tripping a little over her own two feet when her gaze landed on Hank Masters. He was talking to the others, and he smiled over something someone said.

He had dimples.

She felt a flutter in her stomach. It had been brief, but it definitely had been there, surprising her. She hadn't felt anything for a man in five years, more than a simple desire that was satisfied with a no-strings-attached one-night stand. She hadn't wanted anything more than that. She was human. A woman with needs like everyone else, but her dreams of romance and love hadn't come back since her abduction. All that had died inside her.

It was hard to dream when in survival mode.

As if drawn to her as well, his gaze locked with hers and his smiled softened. Her pulse quickened and she quickly looked away, noticing Stacy wave her over. Olivia started walking and didn't stop until she reached their table, keeping her gaze firmly locked on her friend.

"Have a seat." Stacy moved over.

"What's going on?" Olivia sat beside Stacy. Not wanting to seem anti-social, she looked around the table and waved at Trent, Zoe, Hank, and a man she'd never met.

"There's been a break in the case," Trent said.

"First things first." Stacy handed Olivia a menu.

Olivia ordered the lobster salad and a glass of wine.

Once she had her drink in hand, Stacy continued. "I want you to meet my colleague, Winston Bass. He works for the same network that I do, but on a much larger scale. I'm local news, and Winston covers the world news from New York City. Winston, this is our medical examiner, Dr. Olivia Jones. Winston is the best. If anyone is going to help us figure this out, it's him."

"Well, thank you, Stacy. I appreciate the vote of confidence." Winston stood and shook Olivia's hand. "It's very nice to meet you, Dr. Jones." He looked like a typical young and hungry evening news anchor. Probably around forty. Tall, dark, and handsome, with a rich, storyteller's voice.

"It's nice to meet you, too, Mr. Bass." Olivia smiled.

"I was just telling the Sheriff that I had barely gotten back from an assignment covering the war in Ukraine when news of The Cattleman Killer possibly emerging from hiding broke. I was on board the second Stacy reached out."

"You and every other network." Trent grunted.

"You can't blame them, Sheriff," Winston said logically. "A serial killer is more than local news, especially one whose case went cold for years."

"Trent doesn't like all the press interfering with his investigation, but I say it pays to have connections." Stacy winked at her husband.

"You're looking for the wrong guy," Olivia said quietly before taking another sip of wine.

All eyes focused on her.

"What makes you say that?" Winston asked.

"The first victim had light-colored hair instead of dark, and we don't know that she was branded or raped. The second victim had the right hair color and actually was branded, but she *wasn't* raped. Also, the first victim was from Connecticut while the second victim was from Maine. And there were two different weapons used to kill both women. The Cattleman Killer used a tire iron with a chip out of it. Why would the killer change his MO?"

"Because I think you're right. He's not the real killer." Winston perused his notes. "He has to be a copycat."

"My thoughts exactly," Olivia said.

"I'm impressed, Dr. Jones. You're very thorough. Why do you think the killer chose The Cattleman Killer to copy?" Winston looked up at Olivia, studying her curiously.

"Stacy said you have news that might help?" Hank asked, saving Olivia from having to reveal her secret identity.

Olivia wilted with relief when everyone turned their attention toward Winston.

"Yes," Winston responded. "I did some digging on the two victims and found a connection."

"Really?" Hank sat up straighter. "Like what?"

"Well, Penelope Kensington was a collector of fine art pieces." Winston flipped through his notes. "As for Fay Allenby, we all know she was the museum director. The shipment she received the day she was murdered contained several pieces of fine art as well. I think art is the connection."

"That's interesting. Nothing was missing after Fay's murder when I double-checked the inventory with Nolan Turner," Zoe chimed in. "Maybe Fay caught the thief in the act, and that's why she was murdered. It was strange that the door was unlocked, though, but Fay had been working late so she probably hadn't locked up yet. Nolan found her the next morning." Zoe looked at the Sheriff. "The Food, Wine, and Art Festival hasn't happened yet. There's still time for another attempt on the art."

"Amp up security over the collection," Trent said.

"Done." Zoe made a note.

"I'll reach out to my contacts and see if there are any leads pertaining to art thefts. If we find the perpetrator, we just might find our copycat killer." Winston pulled out his cell phone and sent a message. He looked up and his gaze shot across the room, transforming his face into a frown. "You have got to be kidding me."

"What?" Stacy followed the direction of his gaze. "Oh, *her*."

They all looked to see who Winston was staring at.

"Lorelai Crawford." Winston sighed. "The lead journalist for my network's biggest competitor. She's going for the anchor position for the world news for her network, same as I am for mine. No matter what story I cover, she turns up, trying to out scoop me."

Lorelai was a tall, leggy brunette with long curly hair. As if she knew he was talking about her, she turned striking emerald-green eyes in their direction. She tipped her full lips up into a wide smile, winked, and sent Winston a little wave.

"Challenge accepted, Lorelai." He saluted her with two fingers and an anchor-worthy smile, then turned back toward Stacy. "In the meantime, I'm at your disposal. I'll be staying at Coldwater Commons. Given that we work for the same network, I think we can get further if we work together and compare notes."

"Sounds great." Stacy let out a big breath of air. "We're so short-staffed right now, it's been difficult covering the murders and sports. Yet another contributor to the conflict of who's getting more attention: the arts or sports. The battle never ends."

"Speaking of the conflict and sports, I questioned the Little League coaches, Derks, Bryce, and Miley," Trent said. "Everyone saw the argument they got into with Fay the day of her murder."

"That's right," Stacy said while nodding. "They were angry that the town's money went toward the art auction coming up instead of new uniforms for the Little League team. They have their own booster club with a fundraising department, so I don't get why they need the town's help."

"What did they say when you questioned them?" Olivia asked.

"They claim to have been in meetings most of the evening, covering for each other at the time Fay was murdered." Trent shrugged. "There's no way to prove otherwise at this time. None of them have a record, but Derks has been known to be a hothead. He's gotten into a few heated arguments with other coaches and some parents."

"I covered The Cattleman Killer's case five years ago," Hank said, drawing all eyes in his direction. "I'll pull the file and see if I can figure out any more clues." Olivia studied Hank, but as always, his expression was unreadable.

"I thought you were from Boston?" Trent raised an eyebrow at him. "Those killings happened in Florida."

"I started out as an FBI profiler in Florida then got transferred to the Boston field office." Hank lifted his hands. "That's why I volunteered to work this case when you reached out to our office. Not sure it will do any good to look at my old files again, but you never know. Sometimes a little time and distance can bring a fresh perspective to a case. I figure it's worth a shot."

"Good," Trent said. "The more we know about this guy, the better."

Their food came, and they all ate in silence.

Olivia didn't know how to feel about Hank having worked The Cattleman Killer's case years ago. It made her feel vulnerable, like he knew way too much about her. Then again, he, more than anyone, could understand what she had gone through.

They locked eyes for a moment and she felt the unmistakable connection between them.

She tore her gaze away and went back to eating her meal, deciding to focus on the positive and not worry about the rest. She had more friends here than she'd had in years. Maybe working together, they could solve these murders and put a bad guy away. The copycat killer might not be The Cattleman Killer, but he was a killer just the same.

For the first time in a long time, she didn't feel so alone.

6

Spring Fest drew a good-sized crowd, despite the murder investigations, thanks to Garcia Events. The man had lived up to the hype about his talents. Jack was a volunteer every year. The farmers' market was in full swing on the edge of town, with live music, workshops, and crafts he'd helped set up.

Wagon and pony rides were given at some of the local dairy farms. Demonstrations of taking care of cows, milk production, making consumable dairy products, breeding, and calving, among others, were held. Most importantly, delicious samples were shared.

Jack liked the parade most of all. He was a volunteer firefighter, so he helped to build and agreed to ride on the firehouse float. Deputy Zoe Granger was one tough cookie. She didn't mind getting her hands dirty and sure wasn't afraid of hard work. She volunteered as well in most of the things that he did, giving him a chance to get to know her better.

She would discuss many subjects with enthusiasm and knew a little bit about a lot of things. He liked that. He liked *her*. He hadn't planned on getting involved with anyone after his last attempt at dating had failed so miserably, but Zoe wasn't just anyone.

She was different.

Always up for a challenge, she loved to compete with him. He had fun with her, but she seemed to be oblivious to his flirting. Every time he asked her out, she treated the *date* as if they were just friends, sometimes even inviting others to join them. He didn't know what else to do to get through to her.

"Hey, Ross, get your head back in the game," Zoe hollered from the police float in front of his.

His gaze snapped up to hers, and he forgot what he was going to say.

She adjusted her hat, looking sharp in her uniform, and then raised a pale-blonde eyebrow at him. "The parade's about to start, man. What's the matter with you?"

"Just daydreaming, darlin'." He winked at her.

She rolled her eyes at him. "Get your head out of the clouds."

"Aye aye, captain." He saluted her and grinned.

"That ship has sailed, pal. Let's roll." She took her place as the engines to all the floats started.

Jack did the same, and the floats began to move through the crowded streets. He wondered what had really happened when she was a part of the Coast Guard. He'd tried to talk to her about it a couple of times, but she always changed the subject. Yet it was clear she loved the water. He found her at its edge most days, but she refused to step foot on a boat again.

Maybe if he could help her with that, they just might stand a chance.

* * *

ZOE WAVED TO THE LOCALS, tourists, and media alike, throwing candy to children. She watched Jack do the same as they slowly crawled down Main Street, all the way to the harbor, where the parade ended at the marina. It was a beautiful day. The sun was shining bright with no clouds in the sky, and a warm breeze was blowing in off the ocean.

She loved the water so much. A part of her soul had dried up when she quit the Coast Guard. She'd tried a couple of times to get back on a boat of any kind, but she couldn't bring herself to do it. So, she'd settled for living in a harbor town and spending time on its docks.

That was about as close as she could get to her old life.

Since Jack owned The Claw and lived in the apartment above it, she saw him every day. She ate at the pub for at least one meal every day, and when he saw her on the docks, he would join her. She'd gotten to know him pretty well in such a short amount of time. It was almost as if they'd been friends their whole lives.

It scared the hell out of her.

She knew exactly what he was trying to do when he flirted with her, but she couldn't go down that road again, no matter how much he was her type. Dirty-blond wavy hair that was too long, sea-green eyes framed with thick lashes, and an athletic body that was tall enough to make her weak in the knees. She would never tell him that, of course.

Loving someone only led to heartache.

Coldwater Cove was supposed to be her fresh start. New job, new friends, new life. Jack was a great guy. One of the best she had met. She couldn't deny there were sparks between them, but she would not jeopardize their friendship by crossing any lines. She looked back at his float, and he was watching her. He was always watching her, and it was getting harder and harder to look away.

She shot him a quick wave, then tore her gaze away. Tents with food and drink samples from all the restaurants in the area filled the marina, as live entertainment played on the dock. After parking the floats, everyone climbed down to join in the festivities.

"Hey, want to grab some food?" Jack caught up to her.

"Sure, let's tell the others and—"

He snagged her arm. "Can it just be us this time?" His eyes were pleading with her, and she didn't have the heart to turn him down again.

"All right, I guess." She crossed her arms in front of her in a fleeting effort to protect her heart, but she was fully aware it was a losing battle.

"Great." His face blossomed with hope, and she had a moment of doubt. "Let's grab some food and take it out on my boat."

"No!" she blurted, struggling not to let her anxiety develop into a full-blown panic attack. She took several slow, deep breaths.

"Hey, it's okay. I've got you." His eyes softened as he touched her shoulder. "Baby steps. But one of these days I'm going to get you to say *yes*."

"That will never happen." They were talking about more than stepping foot on a boat again, and they both knew it.

"Never say never." He winked.

And just like that she felt herself slipping all over again.

* * *

HANK SCANNED THE MARINA, keeping watch. Always alert. With so many people in town, it would be easy for another attack to happen. Someone could get snatched and dragged into the woods without anyone realizing it amidst all the noise and commotion going on. He knew the town needed money, but continuing with the festivals wasn't smart, given the gravity of the situation they were all in.

A killer was most likely in the marina right now.

Earlier today Trent and his deputy, Zoe, rode on their parade float while Jack and the fire department rode on theirs. The mayor's office, town council members, school board members, and local organization officials all had floats of their own as well. Remy watched over the harbor and docks, while Larry was present in case anything went wrong with the sound system or food tent mechanics.

That only left Hank to keep watch over the crowd.

And watch he did, now that everyone was congregating in the marina. A certain captivating medical examiner stood talking to Stacy and Trent now that the parade had ended. Hank made his way over to join them, passing Jack and Zoe along the way as they carried plates of food over to the dock by the band. He waved to them, but they only had eyes for each other. He'd seen that one coming.

Hell, the whole town had.

Garcia and his crew made the rounds, keeping everything on track. Laura spoke to him for a moment before joining her husband and twins by the games section of entertainment. Local media were covering the festival, while all sorts of other media were still in town covering the murders.

Winston and Lorelai looked like a married couple, sparring and one-upping each other all day. They may pretend not to like each other, but no one could deny the sparks flying between them. With camera crews and microphones everywhere, it was difficult for Hank to have his eye on everyone, keeping him on edge.

"How's everything looking?" Trent's face revealed a mask of concern. He'd done his duty as sheriff by participating in the town events, but the stress of the murder investigations was obviously taking its toll.

"Good so far." Hank nodded. "I haven't seen anything unusually suspicious."

"Thanks for helping out." Trent shook his hand. "I appreciate it, man."

"Not a problem. I'm not here just to sit behind a desk profiling a killer." Speaking of sparks, Hank's gaze drifted to Olivia. "I don't want to see anyone else get hurt."

"Cheers to that." Olivia held up her drink and then took a sip, her eyes not quite meeting his as the women joined their conversation.

"So, what are your plans for the rest of the evening?" Stacy asked her.

"David Garcia asked me to go for coffee later." Olivia shrugged.

Hank arched a brow.

Her gaze shot to his for a second before she continued. "He seems like a nice enough guy, but I'm just not interested in him that way."

Hank let out the breath he hadn't realized he'd been holding.

"I told him maybe some other time because I didn't want to make him feel bad. I said I had work to do in the lab, which is true. There's still so much work to do in my mess of an office as well."

"Work? What's this I hear about work?" Tia came to a stop by Olivia with her brothers. "You know what they say about all work and no play. You should join us for dinner. Right guys?" She looked at her brothers.

"Sounds fine to me." Calvin smiled.

Dijon shrugged. "I mean, you have to eat, so why not. Right?" He looked Olivia in the eyes and held her gaze.

Hank ground his teeth.

The dude was clean cut and dressed to the max. They all were. The Johnson family had good genes, that was for sure. Hank unbuttoned his sport coat, uncomfortably. His usual attire was a pair of jeans, nice shoes, a t-shirt and sport coat, no tie. He was a confident man when it came to his appearance, but this trio was intimidating.

They dressed like they were celebrity realtors.

"Well, if you all don't mind, that sounds nice," Olivia responded.

That got Hank's attention.

"Yay!" Tia clapped her hands. "I'm so happy you're joining us. I worry about you being all alone out in the woods."

"I'm fine but thank you. You're a good friend." Olivia reached out and squeezed Tia's hand. "So, where are we going?"

"Well, Calvin and I have a showing at six tonight in the next town. There's a really nice French restaurant I have been dying to try there."

"Oh, shoot. My car died in the parking lot as soon as I got here this morning. I had it towed to the shop. If we were eating local, I was just going to walk there." She looked thoughtful. "I can always find a ride."

"That's not smart with a killer on the loose," Hank interjected, uneasiness filling him. "I'll drive you."

"That won't be necessary." Dijon's gaze never left Olivia's face. "I'll pick you up at seven, if that's okay."

"Are you sure you don't mind?" Olivia looked surprised.

"Not at all. It would be my pleasure." He tilted his head to the side in a nod. "I'll get your number from Tia and text you when I'm on my way."

"Okay, then, it's a date." Tia grinned wide, showing pearly white teeth. "Come on, Calvin, we have to get ready for the showing."

Olivia blinked.

Hank frowned.

"See you at seven." Dijon caught up to his siblings and the trio left, leaving behind a whirlwind of emotions in their wake.

"Ugh, what now?" Olivia quickly said, looking beyond Hank with worry lines creasing her brow. "Here comes David Garcia right for me."

"Must be he thinks now is later," Stacy said.

Hank didn't think, he just acted. Grabbing Olivia's hand, he walked with her right past Garcia, who met his eyes with a scowl but didn't say a word. Hank didn't stop until he reached his car. Even then he took a moment before he let go of her hand.

"May I give you a ride home?" He tried to keep the urgency out of his voice, not wanting to sound desperate. He didn't know what had come over him. Now was not the time to get involved with a woman, but Olivia wasn't just any woman.

She was *her*.

And he was jealous as hell.

She surprised him by saying softly, "I would like that very much."

* * *

THIS DAY RANKED at the top of Olivia's list as one of the craziest.

First, her car died in the morning. This was not the time to be without a car. Then David Garcia had asked her out. She'd said *no* because she had to work, which was true, but she also just wasn't that into him. Then Dijon had offered to pick her up for dinner with his siblings, which David got wind of and wasn't happy about.

Next, Hank, whom she couldn't quite figure out but

was *definitely* into, had given her a ride home from the festival. He'd insisted on checking out her place to make sure everything was safe. They'd exchanged a few heated glances, and then he'd abruptly left.

David Garcia had shown up unexpectedly, which freaked her out that he knew where she lived. But he'd brought her a homemade dessert he had made and planned to give her when they went on their coffee date, making her feel even worse. She was pretty sure he just didn't like hearing *no* for an answer, but she did feel bad about turning him down only to say *yes* to someone else. He seemed harmless enough, so she'd put on a pot of coffee and invited him in. He'd stayed for a while, making small talk, and then he left, which was the reason she wasn't ready on time.

Dijon showed up early to pick her up for dinner, so she had him come inside to wait while she finished getting ready. He was Tia's brother, so she wasn't worried about him being in her house. He was an attractive man as well, but so intense and mysterious. She didn't need either of those in her life right now. The car ride had been awkward, but once she was with Tia, everything had gone smoothly.

She'd asked Tia to give her a ride home just so there was no confusion for Dijon. She didn't want him to think that this had been an actual date for them. It had been a *family* dinner date with a friend, and that was all.

She did *not* need him to try to lean in for a good-night kiss.

"You are one hot commodity, my friend." Tia pulled into Olivia's driveway and cut the engine.

"I don't know what you're talking about." Olivia played dumb.

"Yeah, right. First, Garcia is all into you. He's one well-put-together man."

Olivia shook her head. "But not my type." He was a

little too full of himself. She'd caught him flirting with *several* women in town, not just her.

"Well, he's sure into you." Tia raised her eyebrows.

"Because I'm the only woman in town who is shorter than him. Although, he seems to like them all. He's good looking enough. I'm just not into love quadrilaterals, or however many women are in his life."

They both laughed.

"You have a point there. On to my second point. My brother has a big ole crush on you." Tia watched her closely.

"Your brother is definitely way more my type, but I'm not interested in dating anyone right now," Olivia said, adding softly, "I haven't dated seriously in a long time."

"Understood." Tia's eyes filled with compassion as she added just as softly, "One of these days I hope you'll tell me about that."

Olivia raised her finger and made a check motion in response but didn't say a word.

"Then there's my third point. That hunky special agent FBI guy. You can't tell me *he's* not your type. Honey, he's everyone's type."

"Yes, he is, but even if I was ready for romance again, he looks like he's in pain to be around me. I don't think he wants romance any more than I do."

Tia tsked. "Oh, Lordy, you two have issues."

Olivia raised her hands, not arguing with her friend because it was true. "All the more reason not to get involved with each other."

"Whatever you say, honey." Tia started her car again. "I have an early showing. You going to be alright here alone?"

"Aw, thanks for caring about me, but this is my home. I have to be okay alone. Now, stop worrying about me," Olivia said teasingly, adding with a smile,

"Thanks for the ride." She got out of the car and closed the door.

"Anytime, love. I'll see you tomorrow," Tia said through the open window.

Olivia waved as Tia left and let herself into her cottage, locking the door behind her. She headed into her bedroom to change into her pajamas, wanting nothing more than to put an end to this crazy day. Wine and a good book were all she wanted to curl up with tonight.

Opening her dresser drawer, her hand paused. She kept her drawers meticulously neat, like her lab, with every item precisely folded. This drawer was a jumbled mess. She checked all the other drawers, and they had been rummaged through as well.

With her heart beating in her throat, she opened her underwear drawer.

This was the only drawer with every item carefully folded and untouched. That was how it made it so easy to notice. There was a big, bare, gaping hole right in the middle where a pair of her lace panties should be.

She left the drawer open, yanking her hand back as if she'd been burned, and called the first person she thought of.

"Masters here."

"H-Hank? Can you c-come over right now?"

"Olivia? What's wrong."

"I think the killer was in my house."

"Be there in ten minutes. Don't let anyone in but me." He hung up, and the line went dead.

Wrapping her arms around herself to ward off the chill that had settled deep into her bones, she clutched her cross necklace and prepared herself for the longest ten minutes of her life. One thing was certain...

She was definitely not okay.

7

"WHAT HAPPENED?" Hank sat at the kitchen table in Olivia's cottage, his heart still beating faster than it should.

He'd been getting ready for bed after poring over his folder on The Cattleman Killer for hours, looking for anything at all he might have missed five years ago. Anything he could add to the killer's profile. He didn't think they were dealing with the same person. These murders were too different. But still, he didn't want to overlook anything that might help these current cases. When Olivia called, adrenaline had surged through him over her words.

I think the killer was in my house.

He'd grabbed his keys and taken off, still wearing his charcoal gray FBI sweatpants and matching t-shirt. It had been awkward standing in her bedroom, looking in her underwear drawer. He didn't trust himself to sit beside her on the sofa in her living room. So, he'd suggested she put on a pot of coffee and sat across from her at her kitchen table.

She'd poured them both a stiff drink instead. He had to admit they each could use one. The thought of someone being in her place, going through her things, stealing something so personal, and terrorizing her filled him with fury.

Someone was playing games with her, and he wanted to know why.

She inhaled a shaky breath, her hair loose from its normal braid, falling in a silky waterfall over the front of her shoulders all the way to her waist. She didn't have any makeup on. She didn't need any. Her skin was flawless, and her stormy gray eyes were framed with thick black lashes. She wore black yoga pants and a soft light purple sweatshirt. It wasn't cold out, but she looked chilled.

She took a sip of her whisky, then looked him in the eye. "After you dropped me off this afternoon, David Garcia showed up."

Hank frowned. "For what?"

"He had asked me to go for coffee, but I turned him down because of work. Then I agreed to dinner with the Johnsons and accepted a ride home from you. I don't think David was too happy about that, and I felt bad. So, when he showed up to drop off the dessert he had made for me, I invited him in for coffee."

Hank's heart did a funny little flip. "Why would you do that? You don't know him. He could be a bad guy."

She thrust out her chin. "I don't know you, either."

"I have a badge to prove I'm a good guy." He clenched his teeth, and a muscle in his jaw bulged.

"In my experience, some of the worst people are law enforcement officials." She tossed back the rest of her whisky and winced.

He raised an eyebrow. "I can assure you I'm not one of them." He downed the rest of his own whisky without so much as a flinch.

She sighed. "Anyway, after he left, Dijon Johnson showed up early to pick me up for dinner. I wasn't ready yet, so I invited him inside to wait while I finished up."

"Of course you did," Hank muttered, getting irrationally irritated over the attention she was getting from the men in town. It was none of his business who she did or didn't date. He just had to keep reminding himself of that, and he would be good.

"Do you want to hear the rest of what happened or not?" she snapped, obviously having heard him. "Maybe I should have called Sheriff West instead."

Frankly, he was surprised that she had called him instead of Trent, but he wasn't complaining. "My apologies." He took a moment to check himself. "You don't know Johnson any better than you know Garcia, and well, we do have a killer walking around," he said carefully. "Did you leave either of them alone while they were there?"

"Yes, both of them. I used the bathroom briefly."

"All I'm saying is you might want to be a bit more careful. Tonight is a perfect example of why. Either one of those men had access to your underwear drawer."

"So did you when you dropped me off in the afternoon," she said without hesitation, looking him square in the eye. "You swept my house before you let me come in, remember?"

"Touché." He bit back a smile over her quick wit. She might be quiet, but underneath, she was a fighter. It reminded him of how tough she had been before and that maybe he should worry a little less about her. "Anything else you care to tell me about this evening?"

Her eyes met his. "You're not going to like it."

So much for not worrying. "Lay it on me."

"When I checked the window to my bedroom, it was unlocked."

He was already shaking his head, not understanding

how she could be so careless. "I don't even know how to respond to that."

"I could have sworn I locked it, but maybe I didn't. For all I know, it could have been the killer who snuck in while I was away at dinner."

"Glad we agree on something."

She wrapped her arms around herself. "Why is this happening?"

"Whoever is doing this is trying to mess with your head. They purposely wanted you to see what they did. To know they were here. Invading your personal space. Touching your things."

"That's so creepy and violating." She shuddered.

"I agree. They must have recognized you early on and decided to copy The Cattleman Killer. Now they're trying to make it look like they're the real killer by tormenting you because they know you were Lilly Swanson, the only woman to get away. If the press finds out who you really are, they will have a field day with the news."

"I couldn't handle that. I can't be in the news again. We need to figure out who this person is and stop them, so I can have my life back."

"Maybe it has something to do with art, like Winston said. He told Stacy his sources found an art theft smuggling ring happening up and down the coast. The copycats obviously want to divert attention away from what they're really doing."

"Wow, that makes sense. I hadn't really thought of it like that."

"We figure that out, then the murders will stop."

Olivia yawned, looking exhausted. "How can I help?"

"Lock your windows and doors and quit letting people in," he said flatly.

"Including you?" She smirked.

"Oh, I'm not going anywhere." He stared her down.

Her smirk vanished and eyes widened.

"For tonight, anyway." He looked away from her gaze. "I'll take the couch."

She hesitated for only a moment. "Thank you, Agent Masters. I don't think I could sleep a wink if you left."

He nodded and watched her walk away, taking her lavender and mint scent with her. She entered her bedroom and left the door open a crack. Something told him he wasn't going to sleep *a wink* any time soon.

* * *

"THIS IS STACY WEST, reporting to you live from the Little League baseball fields, here in Coldwater Cove." Stacy stood beside head coach Derks Callaway and his assistant coaches Miley Hart and Bryce Ferrone. His team and their families were all in the background, celebrating their latest win. "Coach Callaway, it's good to see you."

"It's good to be seen, Mrs. West. These kids have worked long and hard to get where they are today. *They* deserve to be seen." Derks swept a hand in their direction and then adjusted his baseball hat.

"Well said. And soon the whole world might be seeing them. Congratulations on making it this far in the playoffs." Stacy looked into the camera. "Only one more game to go to determine who will be moving on to a spot in the Little League World Series. How exciting!" She looked back at the head coach. "Good luck to you all."

"Thank you, but we don't need luck," Bryce interjected. "We're not worried, right Coach?" Derks nodded. "These kids *will* win the final game. They've earned a spot in the series. You can bank on that."

"You know what they say about overconfidence. Nothing is a sure thing. What happens if you don't win?" Stacy stuck her microphone out closer to the coaches.

"Our star pitcher, Rosy Rodriguez, is on fire," Miley said with confidence. "She'll make it happen. She always gets the job done."

"That's a lot of pressure, especially for a twelve-year-old," Stacy commented, trying to keep the frown from her face.

"Pressure never hurt anyone, Mrs. West." Derks looked directly into the camera. "Maybe someone should put a little pressure on the mayor to spend the town's money on new uniforms for these kids, instead of more festivals. We're taxpayers. We deserve to have a say in how our money is being spent."

"Don't you have a booster club, Mr. Calloway?"

He stiffened. "Little League is expensive, Mrs. West. There's travel, food, lodging, fields to maintain, and yes, uniforms. We need the town's help."

"I'm sure Mayor Flemming is doing her best in light of the winter storm damage and recent murder investigations." Stacy was finding it hard to keep her opinions to herself. They were talking about her best friend here, and Derks was known for being a hothead, always trying to stir the pot.

"Well, I'm not so sure her best is good enough, in light of a once-in-a-lifetime chance to make it to the World Series. Being an athlete yourself, I would think you would understand." Derks narrowed his eyes.

"I understand Coldwater Cove has many needs that require money," Stacy said diplomatically, adding, "Uniforms are a luxury. Rebuilding our town is a necessity. Fulfilling all the town's needs will involve the whole community coming together."

"I'm glad you said that." He looked into the camera

once more. "If you support our young athletes, stop by our field and sign the petition going around for new uniforms. It's our time to shine, people. Let's make this happen."

Oh, boy. "Well, there you have it. Lots of things are happening in Coldwater Cove these days, so stay tuned. Back to you, Ken." Stacy smiled for the camera until they gave her the sign they were off the air, then her lips formed a flat line.

She was about to tell these coaches what she really thought.

Just then, the overcast sky opened up and rain started to fall. Stacy ran for the news van with one thought on her mind…

Mayor Flemming was *not* going to like this one bit.

* * *

EARLY THE NEXT morning Olivia was having breakfast at The Lost Horizon with Stacy, Zoe, and Laura. The four of them had become good friends. Tia wasn't a morning person and didn't eat breakfast unless she was with a client, but she had gotten to know them all as well. For the first time in a long time, Olivia had *real* friends, not just colleagues or acquaintances.

She was getting closer to trusting them but wasn't completely there yet. Tia was the only one who knew about Olivia smelling the fantom men's cologne. Hank was the only one who knew about someone stealing her underwear. And Trent and Hank were the only two who knew she used to be Lilly Swanson, the only victim to escape The Cattleman Killer.

She couldn't risk her face being all over the news again.

Right now, they were dealing with a copycat. She didn't know what she would do if the real killer found out where she was and came back to finish what he'd started five years ago. Bile hit the back of her throat, and she pushed her plate of scrambled eggs away.

"Olivia, are you okay?" Stacy asked. "You look a little green."

"I'm fine. Just a little indigestion. But thank you for asking." She picked up her hot tea and took a sip.

"Of course." Stacy smiled.

"I know a certain someone who might make you feel better," Zoe said with a twinkle in her eye. "You've been spending a lot of time with Hank Masters."

Olivia's stomach fluttered, and she could feel her face heat. "I'm just helping him with the case, that's all." He was the only man she had felt chemistry with in a very long time. She didn't think she could ever feel this way again, but he was so hard to read. He acted interested at times, but then he would put a wall up.

She still felt like there was something he was hiding from her.

"You should talk." Laura laughed, staring Zoe down. "A certain pub owner seems to be occupying a lot of your time these days."

Zoe's grin vanished. "We're just friends."

"If you say so." Laura winked at her, and Zoe blushed.

"Well, I for one, hope both of you find someone special." Stacy smiled dreamily and rubbed her stomach.

"It's the baby talking," Laura said on a laugh.

"Hey!" Stacy swatted her.

"I'm just saying I should know. Believe me, I was the same way when I was pregnant with the twins. I just loved love and wanted everyone to be happy."

"Speaking of love, or a lack thereof," Stacy said. "Coach Callaway and his crew certainly don't have any love for you."

"No kidding." Laura grew serious. "He got more

people than I expected to sign that petition for new uniforms, but it's not enough to force anything. They need to elect a new booster team if you ask me. I understand making the Little League World Series is a big deal, but they still have one more game to win. And even if they do make it, their current uniforms aren't that bad. I simply can't justify allocating funds for that when we still have so much damage to fix after that record-breaking nor'easter."

"What are you going to do about it?" Zoe asked.

"Well, after the festivals are over, I had planned on holding a fundraiser to help his team out. People can't afford to support more than one money-making event at a time. If he could just be patient and wait his turn, things might work out for him, even though I still think there is nothing wrong with the uniforms they already have."

"He makes it hard for anyone to want to help him." Stacy took a sip of her hot chocolate. "No one likes a bully. I feel bad for the kids. He puts a lot of pressure on them, especially on that poor little girl pitcher, Rosy."

"Not to mention, the way he's always arguing with parents and other coaches is an embarrassment to our town." Laura drew her brows together. "It makes me not want to call attention to him as a representative of Coldwater Cove. We already have two murders that happened. This town doesn't need any more negative publicity."

Zoe's phone rang. "Deputy Granger here."

They all watched her as she listened intently, her face hardening.

"I'm on my way." She hung up.

"Who was that?" Stacy asked.

"Your husband." Zoe gave Stacy a meaningful look and then glanced at Laura with a wince.

"What happened?" Laura asked.

"The Town Hall's warehouse in the marina was broken into." A muscle in Zoe's jaw bulged. "Remy heard the commotion and went to investigate when someone jumped him from behind and knocked him out. Larry discovered him and called Trent."

"Oh, no. Poor Remy. I hope he's okay." Laura's face paled. "Please don't tell me that means what I think it does."

Zoe shrugged. "I'm not sure. Sorry, Laura. All the Sheriff said was the warehouse was broken into and Remy was jumped."

"Who would do such a thing?" Olivia wondered what else could possibly happen in this town she had thought would be safe.

"I can take a guess." Anger laced Laura's tone as she pushed her chair back and stood. "The question is, can I prove it. My supplies for the Moose Fest better still be there."

"Only one way to find out." Stacy stood as well.

"You guys are coming with me?" Laura blinked.

"We're a team. You're the mayor, I'm the press, Zoe is the deputy, and Olivia is the coroner. Four heads are better than one in my book."

Laura wilted in relief. "You have no idea how much that means to me."

"That's what friends are for," Olivia said and meant every word.

They all left money on the table for their breakfast and followed Deputy Granger out the door.

8

Hank arrived at Coldwater Cove Marina, cutting the engine to his truck, and climbing out. He walked over to the dock by the harbormaster office and a big warehouse. He'd heard the news over his police scanner and had left immediately. The incident might not have anything to do with the murder investigations, but he liked and respected Trent and was there to assist him in any way.

Trent, Zoe, Stacy, Laura, and Olivia were all sitting in a circle on the grass around Larry and Remy, in front of the open door to the warehouse. Jack came out of The Claw with an ice pack and handed it to Remy, who swapped it with the one he was holding to his head. The sound of sirens wailing could be heard in the distance.

"Remy, will you repeat what you just told me to Agent Masters to bring him up to speed?" Trent pointed to Hank.

Hank pulled a small notebook and pen out of the pocket of his sport coat. "Go ahead, Mr. Finkelstein. I'm ready when you are."

The side of Remy's face was already turning black and blue and beginning to swell. He took a shaky breath. "I was in my office, working early this morning, when I heard a commotion out on the docks. The sun wasn't even up yet. I'm the only one with a key, other than the mayor, for the town's warehouse. I set out to investigate when I noticed the door had been pried open. A flashlight was on, but when I drew close, it went off." Remy swallowed hard.

"Take your time," Hank said.

"I don't remember much after that." Remy looked at Larry who sat beside him.

"I was working early on the docks, helping a buddy out with his boat engine." Larry glanced at Hank. "Being the only maintenance man in town, my days are busy, so early morning is the only time I'm free. I'm just glad I was in the right place at the right time." His face hardened. "I heard the commotion, too, and was just about to go check it out when I saw them jump Remy."

"Them?" Hank's eyebrows drew together.

"It was dawn, and the sky has been overcast with darkening clouds all morning, but I'm pretty sure I saw three shadows. I heard mumbled voices, then a scuffle, followed by a yelp and a thud. I scrambled off the boat as quickly as I could, but by the time I got there, they were gone. Remy lay on the ground with his head bleeding and a tire iron beside him." Larry blew out a long slow breath. "For a moment, I thought he had been murdered like the others."

"Unlikely, since he's a man," Olivia said quietly.

All eyes turned in her direction.

She blushed. "I mean, I'm just saying the killer or copycat probably wouldn't change his MO this late in the game." She shrugged, folding her hands in her lap. "That's all."

"True." Trent's lips tipped down. "But Remy still could have been killed by the blow. He got lucky."

"When I woke up, Larry was kneeling over me. I

couldn't remember a thing." Remy looked at the ambulance with relief as it pulled into the marina and came to a stop beside the group.

"I explained what I had seen to Remy and then called you. I probably should have called the ambulance first, but I was distracted by trying to figure out who would do such a thing. Sorry, Remy," Larry said.

"It's okay. They're here now," Remy replied.

Larry glanced at the warehouse. "I poked my head in there to see what the culprits were after." His gaze shot to Laura's. "You're not gonna like what you find, Mayor."

Laura scrambled to her feet, but Trent grabbed her arm. "Wait. We don't want to disturb any evidence." He looked at the maintenance man and harbormaster. "If either of you remember anything more, don't hesitate to let me know." Trent handed Larry and Remy his card and stepped back to let the EMT's do their job.

"Thanks, Sheriff." Remy left in the ambulance.

"If you're done with me, Sheriff, I need to finish this job before the rain comes so I can start my day. I'm already behind." Larry looked at both Trent and Hank.

"Thanks for your help, Larry." Trent clapped the man on the shoulder.

"Thank you, Mr. Shaw." Hank shook his hand.

"My pleasure." Larry nodded to them and waved to the women before heading back to a boat in the harbor.

"Now can we go check out the warehouse?" Laura asked as the first sounds of thunder rumbled overhead.

"Yes, but let Agent Masters and me lead the way." Trent headed into the warehouse with long, purposeful strides.

Hank was right behind him.

Laura, Stacy, and Olivia brought up the rear, followed by Deputy Granger and Jack. Laura let out a gasp when she saw the scene before them. Hank stopped anyone from entering before the forensic team could dust for prints and look for any other evidence.

"There's not a single supply that hasn't been damaged." Laura's jaw bulged, and she clenched her fists. "I can think of three people who would love to sabotage the Moose Fest. If they think they're getting new uniforms now, they have another think coming."

"Other media are showing up. Don't say anything you'll regret." Stacy pulled Laura away from the warehouse door.

"We'll find out who did this, Laura," Trent vowed. "I can promise you that."

"Sheriff, can I see that tire iron Remy was hit with?" Olivia pulled on the rubber gloves she always carried in her bag.

Trent waited for the forensic team to photograph it, then motioned for Olivia to proceed. "What are you thinking?"

She carefully picked up the tire iron, examined it, and breathed a sigh of relief. "There's no chip out of it."

"It could be the copycat's handiwork." Trent made a note in his notebook. "His tire iron didn't have a chip out of it, either."

"I don't think it's the copycat." Hank studied the room. "A lot of people have tire irons. These people weren't after a woman. They were looking for something specific, or they were out to stir up trouble like the mayor said." He glanced over at Laura and Stacy, who were talking to Winston and Lorelai.

More thunder rumbled.

"Or they were looking for art, if there really is an art connection," Deputy Granger said. "Everyone knows there are several pieces of fine art that are going to be auctioned off during the Food, Wine, and Art Festival. Maybe they thought the mayor had stored them in the warehouse with the other festival supplies."

"That's a good point, Deputy Granger," Hank said.

"I want a rotating security detail placed at the museum until that festival auction," Trent said to Zoe. "I don't think we put enough security on it the first time."

"You got it." She left.

"I've got to run as well. Lots to do before the lunch crowd rolls in." Jack headed back to The Claw, catching up with Zoe along the way.

"I'll let you know if we find anything as soon as it comes in," Trent said to Hank, as the first flash of lightening zipped across the sky.

"Sounds good. And I'll let you know if I find anything new in my file on The Cattleman Killer. I'm still going through it."

"I'll be in the lab if either of you need me." Olivia waved to Trent and Hank, then started to head for her car.

"I see you got your car fixed." Hank lengthened his pace until he caught up to her.

"Apparently, the spark plugs were detached." She peeked up at him, looking concerned. He'd grown to know her well enough to read her body language.

He frowned. "Spark plugs can become broken, but they don't usually detach on their own."

"That's what I thought." She chewed the inside of her cheek. "Do you think someone tampered with them?"

"It sounds like it. The question is, *why?*" He walked with her all the way to her car, then looked in the front, back, and beneath until he was satisfied no one was hiding in there. "Can you pop the hood? I want to make sure everything is okay with the engine this time."

She opened her car door and got in, then did as he asked.

He studied the engine, but everything looked fine. After closing the hood, he walked over to her door, and she rolled the window down. "Remember what I said about not letting people inside your cottage and keeping the windows and doors locked?"

"Yes." She nodded.

"The same thing goes for your car. Too many suspicious things are happening now. You need to stay alert."

"I will." She paused for a moment, her eyes meeting his and holding him captive as she put her hand over the edge of the door. "Thank you, Hank. For everything you've done for me. It means a lot."

"Of course." He bowed his head, then placed his hand over hers and squeezed lightly. "You take care, Olivia. Maybe I'll see you later."

"You know where I'll be." She smiled a little as she slid her hand from beneath his and slowly rolled up her window before pulling away and leaving the marina.

And leaving Hank's heart unsettled.

* * *

IT WAS the end of a very long day. Olivia had been poring over Clive's old files, adding and removing things that were a mess. On top of that, she had these new murders to finalize the autopsy reports. Full reports took weeks to prepare, and so far, she'd only give her initial assessments. The pressure was starting to get to her.

Glancing at her watch, she decided it was time to call it a day. She packed up her bag and headed outside to her car. The rain was coming down steady, but the storm had mostly passed. She pulled the hood of her raincoat up and dashed towards her car. Fishing her keys out of her bag, she noticed her car was already unlocked. She puckered her brow.

Hank would have a fit.

Confused, she mentally retraced her actions from

the morning. She was positive she had locked her doors before going into work and hadn't gone anywhere the rest of the day, not even for lunch. Her grumbling stomach was proof of that. She would dwell on that later. Right now, she needed to get home and dry. Opening the back door, she went to toss her things in the back seat...

And froze!

A scream lodged in her throat, rendering her speechless. She dropped her things on the ground and covered her gaping mouth with shaking hands.

"Olivia?" Hank had just come out of the Sheriff's office and jogged over to her.

She looked at him, feeling numb, having no clue what to say.

He studied her pupils then gripped her shoulders and shook her a little. "Olivia, talk to me. What happened?"

She blinked, pulling herself out of her shock, and her body started shivering. She pointed to the back seat of her car.

He raised a brow and then looked inside, his eyes springing wide. "Are those what I think those are?"

She nodded. "Yes. Those are my missing underwear."

"I'm guessing they weren't shredded before."

She shook her head and wrapped her arms around herself.

"Did you lock your door like I asked you to?"

She nodded. "But someone got in anyway." She pointed to the wet floormats, squeezing her eyes closed. Five years ago, she'd been kidnapped on a rainy day just like this, and her life had been changed forever.

"It's okay, Olivia. I'm here now, and I'm not going to let anything happen to you." His words enveloped her in a warm embrace, keeping her panic at bay.

She opened her eyes as he put his arm around her and guided her to his truck. Once he helped her into the seat, he ran over to grab her things, then locked her car and made a phone call. When he hung up, he ran back to his truck and drove her home.

It felt like forever, but he finally pulled into the driveway of her cottage. The next thing she knew, they were inside with the door closed and locked tightly behind them. He helped her take her coat and boots off, and she just stood there, staring at him.

She felt so cold inside.

"W-Why is someone doing this to me?" she whispered. "He's trying to mess with my head, and it's working. I can't let any of them have power over me again."

"Hey, look at me." Hank put his hands on her shoulders and dipped his head lower so he could look into her eyes with his deep-blue, mesmerizing ones. "I don't know what game this copycat is playing, but I'm damn-sure going to find out. I won't stop until I put this bastard and his groupies away for good. I can promise you that. We just need to distract you. Take your mind off them. Take your power back."

Hank was so handsome. She wanted to run her hands through those golden blond locks and over his muscular body. Her gaze traced over every inch of his chiseled face, lingering on his full lips.

"What are you doing?" His voice cracked and Adam's apple bobbed.

"Distracting myself," she managed to say, before lifting her hands and flattening them on his chest.

"I don't know if this is such a good idea," he said, his voice sounding husky and eyes filling with desire.

"I'm only doing what you said." She licked her lips. "Taking my power back." She fisted her hands in his shirt and pulled his lips down to hers.

The second their lips touched, they both became frantic, kissing each other deeply in a tangle of arms and legs. Hank lifted her up, and she wrapped her arms and legs around him, touching and tasting as much of him as she could. He was her lifeline. Her savior. She felt warm, protected, and safe with him. As powerful as he looked and felt, the gentleness in his touch was undeniable.

She wanted him more than she could ever remember wanting anyone.

She deepened the kiss, and he pulled back, breathing hard.

"Olivia, are you sure?" His eyes, so full of passion and sincerity, searched hers. "I need to hear you say it."

The fact that he asked her made her heart melt. "Positive. I want you, Hank." She touched his face with her fingertips. "I *need* you."

"Oh, God, I need you, too." His mouth swooped down to hers, and he carried her to the bedroom as his tongue slipped between her lips.

She'd felt lust and desire many times before, but never with this intensity. He set her down and broke the kiss long enough to undress them both. She took a moment to worship the perfection of his body with her eyes and her fingertips. How could muscles that looked so hard feel so incredibly soft. His groan of pleasure, when she trailed her hands lower to stroke the length of him, made her feel powerful and alive.

"Baby, if you keep doing that, this is going to be over with before it starts," he croaked. "My wallet," he managed to say. "Condom is in my wallet."

She bit her bottom lip as she pushed him back on the bed and then snagged his jeans, fishing his wallet out of the pocket. Tossing the jeans aside, she crawled on top of him, his term of endearment making her surprisingly giddy. For the first time in a long time this didn't feel like she was just satisfying a basic human need. It felt like something more. Something deeper.

Something soul-stirring.

From the moment she had met him, she'd felt this strong connection. Like she knew him somehow, which was impossible. They'd never met. Yet his eyes looked so familiar. There was a comfort level she felt with him that she had never felt with another man. Her eyes met his which were burning with need, but he lay still, watching her.

Waiting.

Unwrapping the condom, she rolled it down the impressive length of him. His hands shook as he gripped her hips, but he made no move to take the lead. She loved that about him. He was always thinking of her. She kissed him slowly and ran her fingertips over his chest before finally lowering herself and slipping the length of him inside her.

Her body trembled with need, and she gasped as he filled her completely, making her feel whole. Not damaged or broken. She took a moment to adjust to the sheer size of him, and a tear slipped out of her eye in awe that she could feel this way again.

He reached up and cupped her cheek, looking concerned. "Liv?"

She smiled, saying, "Thank you," before turning her face to kiss his palm, and then she began to move.

Everything else was forgotten as they got lost in each other. Picking up the pace, he followed her lead, running his hands all over her skin until the pressure inside of her peaked and she shouted out his name. He gripped her buttocks as his release followed hers a mere second later. She fell forward and they held each other tight, trembling until the spasms quieted and then relaxed in each other's embrace.

Olivia suddenly realized this was the first time she'd

had sex with the light on, and never once thought of her scar.

"What's wrong?" he whispered, tensing when he felt her tears.

"Nothing. I promise," she rushed to say, stroking her fingers over his muscles until he relaxed once more. "It's just an emotional day."

"I've got you, Liv."

"I'm beginning to believe that." And that was the problem.

9

I WATCHED the little whore fuck another man from outside her bedroom window, just like my ex-fiancé had. She was a beautiful brunette, just graduated from law school, when she decided she was better than me and called off our wedding.

She'd dumped me.

Me!

The one who'd put her through law school. She was an ungrateful little bitch and a slut. She moved on to another man immediately, but I showed her. She was mine. If I couldn't have her, then no one could. I branded her, raped her, and killed her. She was my first, but not my last. It wasn't enough.

She hadn't *paid* enough.

So, I started targeting beautiful, successful brunettes in their late twenties who reminded me of her. Five women. I'd killed four, but one fucking bitch got away... until now.

Disgust filled me. I hated hiding in the woods like a wimp. I wasn't a coward. I wasn't weak. I was strong and dangerous, and that filled me with pleasure. I sighed. I'd promised the other two I would behave for now.

We had a *plan.*

I had to bide my time, but dammit, this was hard. Fury filled my every cell, and I clenched my hands. She wouldn't get away with it. I never let any of them get away with it. They were mine. No one else's. That was why I never let them meet the others. They were mine to tease and torture and kill when I was finished with them.

It had been too long.

I shifted uncomfortably, growing hard. All because of her. I'd had a good thing going until she came along and ruined it all. She'd defied me, and now she was betraying me all over again. She thought I was the copycat killer.

What a joke!

I'd thought the cologne I'd sprayed all over her cottage would be a clue, suffocating her with my signature scent, but it hadn't been. So, I'd upped my game. My wet footprints in the back seat of her car should have been a dead giveaway that it was me.

That I was *back.*

The shredded underwear was a bonus, but she *still* didn't get it. I wasn't some fucking amateur. It was time she started giving me the respect I deserved. I didn't know how much longer I could keep my promise to the others.

"What are you doing out here?" he asked. "You're going to get caught and ruin this for us all."

"You said you would wait until the plan is finalized," she said. "This doesn't look like waiting to me."

"Relax, you two," I said. "I'm just messing with her head. I'm not doing anything to jeopardize our plan. You don't know how difficult this has been for me."

"Yeah, well, your *messing with her head* has drawn more attention from the Sheriff. You need to lay low for a while," he said.

"Don't tell me what to do." I felt the old urge to do harm grow stronger. If they didn't watch it, I just might turn that harm on them.

"Duck! That FBI guy is looking out the window," she said. "We need to get out of here right now and figure the rest out later."

With one last seething look of hatred at the woman in the window, I left the woods thinking, *You can't be protected forever, Princess. The time is coming soon, and you'll be all mine again. And this time you won't escape alive. I can promise you that.*

* * *

"I HAVE to say the hype is right." Laura looked at David Garcia one week later. "You are a miracle worker."

"Not a miracle worker. Just a man who has many friends in high places that owe him." He shrugged, looking pleased with himself. "I called in a few favors."

"Well, I'm a desperate mayor who appreciates the miracle you just pulled off." Laura inhaled a deep breath and exhaled with a huge sense of relief.

"He's being modest." Hannah glanced at David. "He's pretty amazing."

He winked at her.

"I hate to break up this tribute, but we need to brief Larry on the sound system and lighting if you want the evening's entertainment to go according to plan." Jude studied his notebook.

"Well, don't let me stop you." Laura held her hands up. "I have plenty of things I need to finalize as well. You know where to reach me if you need anything."

The trio left and Laura looked around the marina with gratitude, hoping this Moose Fest would be a success and further help Coldwater Cove with all its needs. Everything that had been destroyed had been replaced and then some, launching Moose Mania into full swing.

There was a scavenger hunt all through town to find moose-related items. The person who brought all the items to moose headquarters in the harbor first would be crowned the winner. A weekend away in a cabin in the woods on one of Maine's beautiful lakes was the prize.

The Cove was packed with spectators.

Booths were set up all along Main Street with all sorts of moose-themed crafts. Food trucks lined the harbor with moose-themed entrees, desserts, and drinks. A moose mascot walked around in a moose suit, handing out candy to children. Moose-themed activities were being held in the marina as well.

There was even a moose safari being organized with a caravan of buses, followed by guided hikes to prime moose locations, in hopes of a sighting. And finally, entertainment was lined up for during the day, as well as the evening.

Trent and Hank were patrolling the marina, with Remy back at work in the harbor. Zoe was covering the streets. Jack was helping with the safari. Olivia was volunteering in the craft tents. Stacy was covering the festival news. And Tia was making the most of the situation to hand out her business cards, offering help with business and residential realty as well as vacation rentals, pointing out all the reasons why Coldwater Cove was the place to be.

It took a village to pull everything off, and lucky for Laura, she had one.

Everything had been going amazingly well all day. The town was full of outsiders, which was great. Outsiders spent money. Stacy walked over with Olivia as the sun began to set and the evening activities were gearing up.

"How are you holding up? Are you okay?" Stacy asked Laura as she came to a stop beside her.

"I'm fabulous. Why wouldn't I be?" Laura looked at her best friend curiously, wondering over the wince on her face.

"Because the coaches just got here," Olivia said matter-of-factly, pointing across the marina.

Laura's jaw fell open. "I know they are the ones behind the warehouse vandalism. I can't believe they have the nerve to show their faces here."

"You can't prove it was them," Stacy said gently. "They just won the final Little League game, so they're here celebrating with the team on making the World Series."

"They're going to want new uniforms more than ever now." Laura scowled. "Lucky for them, their shenanigans didn't set the town back. It's only because of Garcia's connections that we were able to pull off this festival. Still, uniforms will be last on my list before seeing to the rest of the town's needs."

"Wow, that's quite the face." Winston joined them, raising his eyebrows at Laura. "I wouldn't want to be on the receiving end of that," he joked.

Laura held up her hand and took a deep breath, counting to ten before relaxing her features. "There. I feel much better. I'm fine now." She pasted on her best smile and hoped they all believed it.

No matter what Stacy said, Laura knew in her gut that the coaches were the ones who had sabotaged her festival. Men like Derks Callaway had such big egos, they couldn't stand not getting their way. And they especially couldn't stand losing to a woman. She might be small, but she was fierce, as he would soon find out.

"Stacy, I was looking for you," Winston continued.

"Did you find anything new from your contacts?"

"Actually, I did. There has been a string of art thefts

up and down the coast. They suspect an art smuggling ring. Northern Maine would be an ideal location, because the water is so deep right up by the shoreline. The boats would never have to pull into the marina for inspection, and the Coast Guard can't patrol everywhere at once."

"That makes sense," Stacy said. "And during the spring, summer, and fall festivals, so many tourists are in town. One could easily store the goods in the woods near the shore and wait for contact to make the exchange. I'll let the Sheriff know to up the patrol of the woods near the coast."

"And I'll make sure Nolan Turner, who was just promoted to the museum art director position, is aware of the situation. He and Deputy Granger must keep the art collection safe at all costs. If anything happens to that, then our biggest festival of all will be a bust." Laura shook her head. "We definitely can't afford that."

"Gotcha!" Lorelai Crawford came to a stop by Winston, poking him in his side.

"Hey!" He rubbed his ribs.

Ignoring his protest, she looked at Laura. "Can't afford what, Mayor?"

Winston rolled his eyes. "None of your business, Crawford."

"Of course, it is," Lorelai said with a cat-that-ate-the-canary smile. "News is everyone's business, darling. You of all people should know that."

"It's on a need-to-know basis. And you, *darling*, don't need to know." Winston grinned back, clearly enjoying himself. He met Laura's gaze, and his message was clear...

Do not say a word to his nemesis.

Stacy's cell phone rang, and Laura breathed a sigh of relief.

"Hi, hon, what's up?" Stacy's eyes widened as she listened, and her mouth gaped open. She slapped a hand over her mouth as she listened some more, then she finally responded, "Okay, hon. I'm on my way." She hung up and looked at Laura.

Laura's heart jumped into her throat. "For Pete's sake, what now?"

"Another dead body was found on the moose safari. Jack just called Trent." Stacy's face turned serious and determined as she looked at Winston. "You coming?"

"I wouldn't miss it." He eyed Lorelai over his shoulder as he took long strides to keep up with Stacy.

"Don't think you're getting rid of me that easily, Bass." Lorelai made haste, hot on his heels.

Olivia spoke to Hank for a moment before joining Stacy, and Hank stayed behind to man the marina. Laura called David and filled him in as she walked. He looked over and gave her the thumbs up that he would hold down the fort. Laura caught up with the others, rethinking her earlier thought...

She was anything but fine.

* * *

OLIVIA STOOD IN HER LAB, pulling on rubber gloves, getting ready to examine the body. Earlier she had ridden with Laura and Stacy to an abandoned shack in the woods. Winston and Lorelai had their own news crews, getting to the shack moments later. Jack said the safari bus drove deep into the woods and then they started the hike. They had sighted a moose with a baby, and everyone was thrilled.

They had just started to head back when Jack noticed a peach silk scarf hanging on a bush off in the distance. He had everyone wait on the trail while he went to investigate. It was a woman's scarf, and it didn't look like it had gone through the winter. It looked to be fairly new. Beyond the bush, he recognized an old, abandoned shack he knew of.

When he headed out to the shack, the smell hit him first. Bracing himself, he opened the door and saw a naked woman, lying on the floor in a pool of blood. He'd barely made it back outside before getting sick and then calling Trent immediately.

As soon as Olivia saw the scene, a paralyzing fear had hit her.

This murder was different from the other two that had happened recently. It had taken her a moment to compose herself before she pronounced the body deceased. As soon as the CSI team was finished, they'd brought the victim to the crime lab. The shack brought back memories Olivia was having a hard time blocking out.

The woman was naked, her body beaten and bruised.

It was difficult not to relive what that felt like, but Olivia had a job to do. She spent the rest of the evening examining her, clarifying what she had suspected. The woman had been in the woods for days. Branded with the letter D. Starved, raped, beaten… and the wound on her head was made by a tire iron with a chip out of it. The exact same MO as The Cattleman Killer.

This was no copycat.

Finishing her exam, Olivia noticed a bulge in the woman's throat. Exploring further, she pulled out a plastic bag with a note inside and nearly dropped it on the floor. Her hands shook so badly when she retrieved the note and read it.

HELLO, *Lilly*…
  You should have thought twice before cheating on me.
  I'm back for what's mine.

You won't get away this time.
Ready or not, here I come!

Olivia did drop the note this time, stumbling back a couple of steps, when suddenly the power went out. She screamed for all she was worth.

Footsteps.

Her breathing started coming in short gasps. Oh, God, she was going into a full-blown panic attack. Trying to keep her wits about her, she made it into her office and fumbled with the drawer to her desk. Pulling out a paper bag, she inhaled slow and deep until her breathing finally regulated and her pulse slowed.

More footsteps right outside her office door this time.

Ducking down behind her desk, she wrapped her hand around her cross necklace and closed her eyes, praying the footsteps would go away. A knock on her door sounded, but she didn't answer. A set of keys rustled, and suddenly the door creaked open slowly.

She held her breath and clutched her cross necklace tighter.

A flashlight shined around the room. "Dr. Jones?" said a man's voice.

Olivia popped up. "Larry?" She looked at the maintenance man and nearly passed out on the floor from relief.

"Sorry, if I scared you." He lowered the flashlight from her eyes. "The power went out all over town, and Sheriff West asked me to head over to the lab and turn the generator on for you. I called out by the lab, but you must not have heard me, so I thought you'd already left. I was just checking your office to be sure."

She let go of her necklace. "I heard footsteps and

panicked a little, that's all." She tried for a smile. "I'm very happy to see you."

"That's understandable, given everything that's been going on lately." He nodded once, his expression sympathetic and sincere. She liked Larry. He made her feel at ease. "If you'll follow me, I'll get that generator back on for you if you want, but it's getting kind of late. Are you sure you want to keep working?"

"I still have a few things to finish up before I can call it a night." She followed him to the door to her lab. "I'm good now. I'll just wait here until you get the generator turned on." She blocked the doorway, not wanting him to see the note on the floor.

He gave her a funny look. "If you're sure you'll be alright, then I'll get to it."

"Yes, I'll be fine. And thank you, Mr. Shaw."

"You can call me Larry, ma'am." He flushed.

Another set of footsteps came jogging down the hall.

Hank appeared with a flashlight in hand, and his other one hovering close to the gun holster beneath his sport coat. He stopped short, eying Larry with thorough scrutiny. "Everything all right here?"

"Just getting the power back on for Dr. Jones," Larry said.

"Olivia." She smiled at him.

"I'll have you right as rain in a jiffy, Olivia." Larry smiled back and then left.

Hank frowned.

"Follow me." Olivia took Hank's flashlight and led the way inside the lab over to the woman's body.

Hank's face paled and he looked away.

She pulled a sheet up over the woman. "You can look now."

He turned back, turning a little green as he cleared

his throat. "I knew you'd still be working, and I panicked when the power went out. Are you okay?"

"That's sweet, and yes. I'm fine… now that you're here." She met his gaze briefly before looking away.

They hadn't really talked about what had happened between them. She knew it had been powerful, and so much more than fulfilling a need, but she didn't know how he felt. So, they'd both acted like it had never happened, going back to business as usual. But *business* had been far from usual since then.

The power surged back on.

Olivia shut the flashlight off and handed it back to Hank. "Here you go."

"Thanks," he said. "We ran a trace on the scarf. It belonged to a Dr. Ali Lambert from Boston. She was in Maine for a medical conference the next town over and disappeared a few days ago. She just turned thirty."

"That fits the real Cattleman Killer's MO. She was branded, starved, raped, beaten, and kept in a shack in the woods for days before he killed her with a tire iron. And this one has a chip out of it."

Hank wrinkled his forehead. "I'm thinking the real killer is in town now, on top of the copycat."

"I don't think." Olivia looked him in the eyes. "I know." She picked up the note on the floor with her gloves and held it up before him.

His face registered shock, then concern, then anger. "I haven't told anyone what happened between us, have you?"

She shook her head *no*.

"Then you know what this means."

She nodded, swallowing hard. "He was watching us."

"Well, hell." Hank scrubbed a hand over his face. "That changes everything."

10

"SEE YOU TOMORROW, EUGENE." Jack waved to the old timer as he walked with a limp out the pub's door.

Eugene had bad knees, a bad shoulder, and a bad hip from all his years fishing. The stubborn old coot refused to have surgery, saying a good shot of whisky was all he needed. How else was he supposed to know when a storm was coming?

Jack chuckled, but his smile faded pretty quickly. He'd seen death before but being the one to find that poor woman in the woods had unnerved him. He couldn't get the image out of his head. He knew there was a copycat killer out there, but to witness the monster's handiwork up close and personal was a whole different matter.

Pouring a double shot of whisky, he tossed it back and winced as it burned its way down his throat. The bar had emptied after the power went out, except for Eugene. The old timer had sat with Jack while he got his generator going, but after Larry got the power back on, Eugene had finally called it a night.

Now that Jack was alone, his thoughts crept in, taking him to a dark place he didn't want to be. He'd had another sister a long time ago. She'd also died way too young. Cold and alone, but at least she hadn't been tortured. The bell chimed over the door, and he looked up. His lips parted, and he slowly exhaled.

Zoe Granger.

"Hey, Jack. You still open?" She looked soft and fresh and *alive*.

"For you, always."

"Good." She ran a hand through her pale, damp strands of hair. "I could use a drink. It's been a hell of a day."

"You're telling me." He scrubbed a hand over his face, then poured her a shot of what he was having.

"You read my mind." She tossed back the shot and hissed out a breath over the burn, then slid her glass back for him to pour her another.

"How do you handle it?" He refilled her glass and slid it back to her.

This time she only took a sip. "Handle what?"

"Death."

Her eyes shot up to his. "Not very well. That's why I'm here. In Coldwater Cove, I mean."

"That's not exactly what I mean, but that explains a lot."

"Oh, you were talking about the dead body you found." She glossed over the death subject, and he let it go.

For now.

"Yeah." He walked around from behind the bar and sat on the stool next to her, swinging to the side so their knees touched, and they faced each other. "I can't get the image of that poor woman out of my mind. Living in these parts and being a volunteer firefighter, I've seen death before. I'm talking about murder. *Torture*. I can't stop thinking about what she must have gone through. How do you get through it?"

"Time." Zoe reached out a hand and touched his

knee. "Murder is never easy. In my line of work, I have to distance myself from it. Look at it objectively, or I would be a mess if I brought my work home with me. My own life is hard enough to deal with."

"You mean your brothers and you getting split up when you were young?"

"That… and losing my fiancé." Her gaze met his and didn't let go.

They'd grown closer every day they'd spent together. She had finally trusted him enough to let him in. He needed to make sure she didn't regret it.

"What happened?" He turned her hand over on his knee and placed his hand on top of hers, palm-to-palm. The heat of her flesh and feel of her soft skin felt comforting. Warm.

Right.

"Alan was a fellow Coasty. We met on a sixty-five-foot cutter down the coast. We fell in love and got engaged, then asked to get transferred up north together. We were so excited to be on a search-and-rescue responder boat together. That had always been our dream. At first, everything was great. We were planning our wedding and saving lives." She squeezed Jack's hand while taking a moment to breathe.

He patiently waited, just holding her hand.

"A storm rolled in, and a couple of fishermen were stranded at sea. We were the closest responder, so we went in pursuit. Alan was always the first one in the water. I manned his safety line and kept a visual. It all happened so fast. A rogue wave hit us, nearly knocking our own boat over. I fell. When I got back on my feet, the safety line had snapped. Alan and the fishermen didn't make it. We looked everywhere, but they were gone. It was all my fault. It was too dangerous. I should have stopped him."

"You couldn't have stopped him any more than I

could have stopped Ellie," he said softly, finally coming to a place where he believed that.

Her glistening pale blue eyes widened. "Who was Ellie?"

"My younger sister. Ellie and Emma were twins. Emma has always loved storms. She went out for a hike, knowing a nor'easter was coming. Ellie didn't like storms, but she refused to let Emma go alone. I told them they were stupid and not to go, but they didn't listen. The storm hit early, and Emma made it back." He shook his head. "Ellie didn't."

"How is that your fault?"

"I should have tried harder to make them stay home. When Emma came home and told us what had happened, I wanted to go out and look for Ellie, but my parents wouldn't let me or Emma. I should have gone anyway. We had to wait until the storm was over before we could look for her. She was curled up in an angelic ball, frozen to death on the ice, and I was never the same again. I was supposed to be the big brother. Their protector. I failed them both."

"That's a lot of pressure you're putting on yourself."

"No more than you in thinking you failed to save your partner."

Zoe looked at him intensely. "H-How did you move forward?"

"It took me a long time to forgive myself and realize there was nothing I could have done to save her."

"I'm trying to get there."

"Talking about it is a start."

Zoe slowly leaned forward and pressed her lips to his. The kiss was soft and warm and perfect, full of everything she couldn't quite say. When she finally pulled away, she smiled tenderly. "Thank you, Jack. We make a pretty good team."

"Thank you, Zoe. We make one hell of a *great* team."

"I know another way to help you get over death," she said, her voice husky and full of passion.

"What's that?" His voice sounded the same.

"You do something that makes you feel alive." She slid off her stool, standing between his legs and wrapping her arms around his neck.

"What exactly did you have in mind, Granger?" His lips were a breath away from hers.

"I have an idea or two, but actions speak louder than words." She walked over and locked the bar door, turning off the open lights, and no more words were necessary.

In three strides, Jack reached her. He picked her up to straddle him and took the stairs to his apartment two at a time, his lips locking with hers and tongue diving deep. She was right.

All thoughts but one had been obliterated from his brain...

* * *

"HEY, DO YOU HAVE A MINUTE?" Hank poked his head inside Trent's office the next morning.

"Sure, what's up?" Trent motioned him inside. He sat behind his desk, going over reports.

Hank closed the door behind him. "You know how the power went out last night?"

"Yeah? I sent Larry over to turn the generator on. We both know how Olivia is. I figured she would be working late, given the discovery of another dead body."

"Exactly. I figured the same, so I rushed over to help."

Trent arched a brow but didn't say anything.

Hank cleared his throat. "Anyway, after Larry left, Olivia pulled me inside the lab to show me something."

"Did you fill her in on who the victim is?"

Hank nodded. "Yes, and Olivia confirmed Dr. Ali Lambert was branded, raped, and then murdered. But this time, the tire iron had a chip out of it."

Trent frowned. "You mean this wasn't the work of the copycat killer?"

"No." Hank shook his head. "And there's more."

"More?" The Sheriff's frown deepened.

A knock on the door sounded, and Olivia walked in the office. She looked at Hank, and her eyes widened briefly. Blinking, she nodded *hello* before she looked back at Trent. "I have the coroner's report for you, Sheriff."

"Thank you, Olivia. Hank was just filling me in." Trent took the folder from her. "He was just telling me you found something more."

Her face flushed pink, and she wouldn't look at Hank as she handed Trent the plastic wrapped note without saying a word.

Hello, Lilly...
You should have thought twice before cheating on me.
I'm back for what's mine.
You won't get away this time.
Ready or not, here I come!

Trent cursed. "You're in more danger than I thought." He scrubbed a hand over his buzz cut. "What the hell is he talking about? You haven't even gone on a date with anyone since you got here, other than with Tia's family, but that wasn't..." Trent's eyes traveled back and forth between Hank and Olivia.

Hank bit back a curse. He'd known getting involved

wasn't a smart idea, especially while working on this case. Olivia looked everywhere except at him.

Trent didn't say his speculations out loud, but he didn't need to. He cleared his voice. "Okay, then." Trent looked back at the note and then at Olivia. "What are we going to do about this? You obviously can't stay alone."

"That's what I tried to tell her last night. Either she stays with me at the hotel, or I move in with her at her cottage." Hank dropped his hands to his hips, shooting a frustrated look at Olivia. "She wouldn't listen to reason."

She raised her chin a notch and tried to stand taller than her five-foot frame would allow. "No one except you two know that I'm Lilly Swanson, the only woman to escape The Cattleman Killer, other than possibly the copycat and real killers. I'm not going to draw attention to myself by shacking up with an FBI agent."

Hank stared at her in disbelief. "I would think that after all we've been through, you would think of me as more than just an FBI agent."

Her rigid posture softened. "I do. I'm just not ready to have my life turned upside down by the media again." She pulled the ends of her sweater over her hands as if cold.

Hank's irritation melted away. All he wanted to do was hold her and comfort her until her fears were gone. At first, he'd wanted to get close to her for a reason, but over time that had changed. He wanted to get close to her now because he cared about her. Falling for her wasn't part of the plan, but damn if he wasn't. Reality hit him hard...

Everything wouldn't be okay when she found out who he really was.

* * *

OLIVIA TOOK a lunch break and met Stacy, Laura, and Zoe at the Lost Horizon. She was so confused. Hank went from acting like nothing had happened between them to acting hurt when she'd referred to him as an FBI agent. If he'd wanted to be something more than that, he hadn't come out and said so directly.

She sighed, reflecting on her thoughts.

Honestly, she wasn't sure what she wanted… other than another night alone together. Being with him had been powerful, but probably not smart. All she knew for certain was that she couldn't stop thinking about being in a very special agent's strong, muscular arms.

"Wow, penny for your thoughts?" Laura said with a chuckle. "You seem a million miles away, and in a very nice place by the looks of it."

Olivia felt her face flush hot.

"I recognize that look," Stacy said with a sly smile. "You're a smitten kitten."

"I don't know what you're talking about." Olivia sat up straighter.

"Give the poor girl a break." Zoe dropped her gaze and pushed her food around her plate. "Just because she looks all dreamy-eyed doesn't have to mean anything happened." Zoe shrugged, her cheeks flushing pink.

"Oh, my Lord, you're just as besotted." Laura clapped her hands. "I was hoping Coldwater Cove would sprinkle its magic on you two."

"Look, we both have come to care about you guys so much," Stacy said. "We just want you to find the same happiness we have. That's all."

"Agent Masters is only in town helping out with the murders." Olivia stopped trying to hide everything. These were her friends. "What am I supposed to do if I fall for him, and then he leaves? I'm used to being on my own. In fact, I prefer it that way."

"That's what I thought when I first came back to

The Cove," Stacy said. "You can't worry about *what ifs*. Life has a way of working itself out."

"Well, I'm all for having a little fun," Zoe said. "Fun doesn't break your heart. I can't risk falling in love again. It hurts too much when that love is taken away."

"You're getting ahead of yourself," Laura added gently. "Quit looking so far into the future, and just live in the moment. Enjoy every day. You've earned some happiness, don't you think?"

"Yeah, we have." Olivia raised her glass. "Cheers to that."

"You know, you're right." Zoe raised her own glass. "I'm done overthinking everything. Cheers to living in the moment. Sometimes a moment is all we get."

They all clinked glasses and went back to finishing their lunch.

Raised voices sounded across the room. Tia sat at a table with David Garcia, having lunch. Hannah was standing in front of them arguing with David. He stood and pulled her off to the side until Jude showed up and got her to leave with him. Tia stood as well, spoke to David with her hands moving as fast as her words, and then walked away.

David paid the bill and then left, looking flustered.

"Are you okay?" Olivia asked as Tia neared their table.

"I've had it with men." She grabbed a chair and joined them.

"What happened?" Laura asked. "David told me he was going to take you to lunch to look for a venue for the Food, Art, and Wine Festival gala."

"Exactly." Tia huffed out a breath. "This was supposed to be a *business* lunch. I actually have a client who rents their barn for events. That would be perfect for the gala."

"Oh, that sounds wonderful," Laura said. "So, what went wrong?"

"Garcia went wrong." Tia scowled. "He changed our business lunch to a romantic one when he hit on me. Granted, we had already finished our business, but still. The man crossed the line."

"Why was his assistant, Hannah, so angry?" Stacy asked.

"I've suspected for a while now that she has a thing for her boss," Laura pointed out. "It's obvious in the way that she looks at him. And he's such a ladies' man, he gives her just enough attention to keep her on the line."

"Exactly." Tia tapped the table, clearly still frustrated. "Hannah and Jude showed up and overheard him asking me out on a date. She flipped out, sounding completely irrational and not making a bit of sense."

"He must be sleeping with her for her to go off like that." Stacy's face registered her disgust for the obvious player.

"I thought the same thing," Tia continued. "David pulled Hannah aside to talk to her, and then Jude got her to leave with him. David tried to explain away what happened to me, saying Hannah was infatuated with him for no reason, but I'd seen and heard enough. I told him I would be dealing with the mayor directly from now on." Tia winced. "I hope you don't mind."

"Good for you," Laura said. "I don't blame you one bit. Garcia Events has done a great job for this town, but I'm glad this is the last of the spring festivals. This town doesn't need any more drama."

"That's for sure," Olivia said, but couldn't help wondering if the drama had only just begun.

11

"WHAT ARE YOU DOING?" Olivia asked later that night as she got out of her car and was unlocking the front door to her cottage.

"If you won't stay with me or someone else, then I will shadow your every move." Hank stood leaning against his truck in her driveway. He'd waited for her to get out of work, and then he followed her home.

Pinching the bridge of her nose, she let out a long sigh. "Don't you think that's a bit overkill?"

Her hair was pulled back in her sensible braid, and she wore functional slacks, a blouse, and shoes, yet she'd never looked more appealing to him. She was special to him, and he would do everything possible to protect her. She looked tired, and he wasn't taking any chances of her letting her guard down and becoming vulnerable to that monster.

"The real Cattleman Killer is not only back... he's *watching* you. So, no, I don't think that's overkill."

She paused a beat, then her shoulders wilted. "You're right."

"Excuse me? What was that again?" He raised a brow at her. "I couldn't possibly have heard you correctly."

Her soft gray eyes met his, and he could see the worry behind them. "I'm tired of being afraid."

His teasing vanished as his heart melted. "Then don't be. I'm here, and I'm not going anywhere."

"Hank, I—"

Hank's cell phone rang. He looked at the caller ID and frowned. "What's up, Sheriff?"

Olivia's eyes widened, filled with questions.

"Be right there." He hung up with Trent and looked around at the dark woods and ocean beyond that, then back at Olivia. "You look tired, but I really don't want to leave you alone out here. You up for a ride?"

"Can I change quick?" Her gaze pleaded with him. "I need to leave the stench of the lab behind me right now."

"Absolutely. Let me go in first. You wait here inside the door." He opened her door and did a sweep of her cottage before motioning her the rest of the way in.

Moments later, she returned with her hair down and brushed, her face washed and free of makeup, and a soft sweatshirt with leggings and sneakers on. She looked refreshed and soft, touchable. He nodded once to her, then led the way outside to his truck before he did something stupid like take her back to bed.

"Where are we going?" she asked, once they were on the road.

"The museum."

"This late?"

He kept his eyes on the road. "There's been another break-in."

She inhaled sharply. "Please tell me there's not another dead body."

"No dead body. Just one shaken-up Museum Director."

They pulled into the parking lot of the museum to a familiar sight these days. Law enforcement agencies,

CSI teams, and media. Stacy, Winston, and Lorelai were interviewing the forensics team and police. Hank guided Olivia over to the Sheriff and Director.

"Hank. Olivia." The Sheriff nodded at them. "Mr. Turner, can you fill Agent Masters and Dr. Jones in on what happened this evening?"

The man ran a hand over his short brown ponytail and then his goatee, seeming unnerved. "You can call me Nolan." He shook his head. "I was the last one here other than the security detail out front. I had just locked the doors and headed for my car when I realized I'd forgotten my satchel. I went back in and heard noises coming from the storage room where we keep the art."

"I thought Deputy Granger had Larry install a security alarm and new locks." Hank looked around. "It doesn't look like anyone broke in. Did the security detail hear anything?"

"No one heard a thing and no one broke in. I always do a sweep of the museum to make sure all the visitors are gone before I lock up. I didn't see anyone, but they must have been hiding out until I closed."

"They?"

"There was definitely more than one voice."

"Was anything taken?"

Nolan's eyes grew somber. "Yes. The art for the Food, Wine, and Art Festival auction. They must have heard me shout out *"who's there?,"* because the noise stopped. I don't like guns, but with a killer on the loose, I grabbed a samurai sword we had on display."

Hank raised an eyebrow at Trent, who narrowed his gaze at Nolan.

"I didn't use it on anyone," Nolan clarified, "but I wasn't about to go into that room unarmed."

"You had one of my men right out front on detail. You should have gone to get him first. That's what he's there for." Trent ran a hand over his face, clearly frustrated.

"I didn't want to waste time going for help," Nolan said defensively. "It didn't matter anyway. When I went in the room, they were gone, and the window was open."

"I don't blame you, Nolan." Olivia picked at a hang-nail, and Hank wanted to hold her hand, but others were watching. "You don't know what these people are capable of."

"Exactly. When Fay was murdered, the front door was unlocked." Nolan looked sad for a moment, but then he pursed his lips before adding, "I thought she was having an affair and that she let her lover in."

"That's not a bad hypothesis. There weren't any signs of a struggle on her," Olivia confirmed, her hands stilling as she focused on the case.

"But now, I wonder if it *wasn't* her lover. Maybe these same people had been hiding out on her, too." Nolan puckered his brow for a moment. "Maybe she didn't struggle because she knew them."

"Were you in love with Fay Allenby?" Hank asked.

Nolan blinked, his lips parting. He snapped them together before answering. "I-I had strong feelings for Fay, yes, but she was my boss. A relationship with her wouldn't have been appropriate."

"No, but it might have angered you to see her having an affair with someone else," Trent speculated.

"An affair was likely, given the evidence showed she had sex, but wasn't raped," Olivia added objectively.

"You said you left before Fay the evening of her murder, and found her the next morning." Trent paced as he talked. "Did you, in fact, forget something that night as well? Maybe you came back and stumbled upon her being intimate with her lover. You waited until her lover left, and then you killed her in a fit of rage, waiting until morning to call the police, claiming to have just discovered her." Trent studied Nolan who had begun to sweat.

"If you couldn't have her, then no one could, and now you have her job. A job that should have been yours in the first place, given your background and that you're older and more experienced than she was," Hank added.

Nolan's face paled. "How do you know that?"

Hank stared him down. "It's my job to know that."

"You're all crazy." Nolan backed up a step.

"Have you heard of The Cattleman Killer?" Trent asked.

"Who hasn't? But why would I choose a killer from Florida who disappeared for years? That doesn't make any sense."

Hank watched him closely, but it was clear either he didn't know who Olivia used to be, or he was one hell of an actor. Hank shot a glance at Olivia, but she had her walls up, her face devoid of emotion.

Nolan threw his hands in the air. "If I had known I would get this kind of scrutiny, I never would have reported the theft."

"Stealing is a crime, Mr. Turner," Trent said. "You had no choice but to report the theft, but I'm not the one you should be afraid of."

Nolan eyed the Sheriff warily. "Who is?"

"Mayor Flemming. Laura is going to be livid when she finds out the art for her auction is gone."

* * *

"THANK YOU." Olivia looked at Hank as they sat on her back patio, having coffee the next morning. It was late spring now, and the days were growing warmer, everything in full bloom, with smells of new growth in the

114

air. The red wine stain was still on her cement, but it had faded considerably.

"Thank me for what?" Hank eyed her curiously, his thick, golden-blond hair messy from sleep. He needed to shave, but he'd never looked better to her. The way that he looked at her with those deep blue eyes melted her heart.

"For staying with me." She cradled her cup of coffee and inhaled the smooth, bold aroma. She was in over her head. Falling for him hard. And she had no idea what to do about it.

"Thank you for letting me." He winked, and her stomach fluttered.

"Sorry I passed out on you last night. I couldn't keep my eyes open."

"You needed to sleep."

She lowered her voice. "You could have slept in my bed."

He hesitated a moment. "Not a good idea. I need to stay alert."

"I have a guest bedroom. You didn't have to sleep on the couch."

"I couldn't afford to get distracted." His gaze slowly traced over her body. "Let's face it, staying anywhere near you is distracting as hell."

She felt her ears heat, so she looked away and blew on her coffee.

He cleared his throat. "The last time I spent the night, I let my guard down."

She looked up at him and met his eyes, seeing his fill with heat and passion. Her gaze dropped to his lips. "Is that so bad?"

"Yes." There was no hesitation in his voice.

That got her attention and had her snapping her gaze back up to his eyes. "Oh, I see." She stood and walked over to the edge of the patio, feeling like a fool.

She felt his presence behind her. "No, you don't see." He wrapped his arms around her from behind and dropped his chin to rest on top of her head. She lifted her hands up and wrapped them around his forearms.

He turned her around to face him. "It wasn't so bad, Liv." She loved when he called her by her nickname. "It was amazing. *You're* amazing. But we can't do that again." He placed a soft kiss on her lips and stepped back from her.

"W-Why not?" she croaked, as her own desires nearly choked her.

He cursed softly. "You have to stop looking at me that way." He walked back to his chair.

"What way?" She licked her lips and did the same.

He groaned and tore his gaze away from her mouth to look out over the water and take a sip of scalding black coffee. "After we made love, I could have sworn I saw someone outside. I know I heard voices." His face hardened. "I know what this *real* monster is capable of." His voice filled with raw emotion. "I'll be damned if I sit back and let it happen again."

"Happen again?" Why did she have a feeling he was talking about something more than just her.

"Last time, I let the case run cold. It was my fault. I owed more than that to all the women who died way too young because of him. I'm going to do better." A muscle in his jaw flexed. "I'm going to stop him for good this time, whatever the cost. I won't let you, or them, down again. I can promise you that."

"Hey." She sat on his lap and took his face in her hands, pressing her lips softly against his. "It's okay."

"No, it's not." He held her tight. "But it will be."

* * *

HANK FOLLOWED OLIVIA TO WORK, and once she was securely in her lab, he headed over to the Sheriff's office. He was falling hard for her. Dammit. How could he have let this happen? After all she had been through, she didn't need him coming in and turning her life upside down. He didn't want to hurt her. He had a job to do.

No matter what, that had to be his number one priority.

He poked his head through the Sheriff's office door. "Hey, Trent. You wanted to see me?"

Trent motioned him in and hung up the phone. "I just got off the phone with a colleague of mine. Bartholomew Vanderholt just confessed."

"Who's that?" Hank sat in a chair across from Trent's desk.

"Penelope Kensington's ex-fiancé."

Hank's brows drew together. "You're telling me *he* murdered her?"

"That's right. She called off their engagement, and he couldn't handle that. He was embarrassed and angry. I guess he's used to getting what he wants, and his ego took a big hit when she left him."

"I bet. Those guys are all alike." Hank ground his teeth before asking, "What did he do to her?"

"He took her out on his boat, they argued, and then he hit her over the head in a fit of rage. She fell off the boat and went under. He tried to find her but couldn't, so he panicked. Not sure if she was alive or dead, he paid people he knew to give him an alibi."

"Of course, he did." Hank clenched his jaw. He was so sick of men who mistreated women.

"Everyone thought she took off somewhere on an adventure. She was known to do that, and had plenty of money. It wasn't until she washed ashore in The Cove that people realized she was not only dead, but had been murdered. Her father hired a top-notch team of investigators who put the clues together that led back to good ole' Bart."

"What about the art connection?"

"There is a string of art thefts happening up and down the coast, and Penelope happens to have a fine art collection, but I'm beginning to think these murders don't have anything to do with that."

"Then why did the collection for the auction get stolen?"

"That's why I called you here." Trent's face grew serious. "That is the million-dollar question we need an answer to."

Hank took off his sport coat. "Then let's get to it."

12

"THIS IS A DISASTER, DAVID." Laura sat across from David Garcia and his assistants at The Claw for dinner. The place was packed as usual. She normally loved the nautical-themed ambiance and classic rock music, but not tonight. She had way too much going on in both her professional and her personal life at the moment.

Tonight, she was on edge.

David held up his hands. "Just calm down. It's not the end of the world. I'll figure something out."

"Calm down?" Laura gaped at him. "Do you know who you're talking to?" The man was a piece of work. He was clearly used to getting his way when it came to women.

He scrubbed a hand over his face, looking more unsettled than she'd ever seen him. "Sorry, Ms. Mayor. It's been a long couple of days."

"So I've heard." Laura glanced over at Tia, who sat with her brothers at a table across the room. They hadn't taken their eyes off him since he came in.

Hannah softly grunted but didn't say a word, her slicked-back, put-together attitude in stark contrast to her actions. She tucked a strand of her short hair behind her hoop-clad ears and pushed her chic glasses up her nose as she stared down at her pad of paper and took notes.

Ken-Doll Jude rolled his eyes in a not-so-subtle way.

"Okay, let me think." David was quiet for a moment before he continued. "I have many connections. Maybe I can get a few people to make donations for the art auction."

"Well, you'd better do something." Laura stared at him, making sure her points sank in. "Tia locked in the Hamilton Barn for the venue, but it won't be much of a gala without the art auction."

"I'm on it. I'll make some calls. A few people owe me some favors. Trust me." David undid the top button of his designer shirt and loosened the collar.

Another grunt sounded from Hannah, and Jude cleared his throat.

Laura narrowed her eyes at them all and then looked at her watch. "All right, well, if that's all, I have the twins' swim meet to get to."

"We'll talk soon." David nodded at Laura and then faced his crew with a muscle bulging from his clenched jaw. "Hannah. Jude. Can you guys stick around? We have a few things we need to get clear."

Laura paid for the meal and left the three at the table with their heads bent together, looking like their conversation had turned intensely serious. She couldn't worry about that now. She had a town to save, no matter the cost. She owed that to Stacy and Stacy's mother, the former mayor, Elizabeth Buchanan, who had been like a mother to Laura as well.

Stopping by Tia's table, Laura smiled at Tia's brothers. "It's good to see you gentlemen. How is our town treating you?"

"Not too bad." Dijon's gaze shot over to Garcia, and his eyes narrowed. "For the most part."

Tia rolled her eyes at Laura, and Laura bit back a chuckle.

"Can't complain," Calvin responded. "People are friendly, and business is picking up, so it's a win-win. If only Tia wasn't such a slacker."

"Hey." Tia smacked him lightly on the arm.

Calvin laughed and shrugged.

"Brothers." Tia shook her head.

"Men." Laura lifted her hands.

They all laughed.

"Seriously, though, I'm glad you're all settling in nicely." Laura looked around the pub at so many faces she knew and adored. People were counting on her, and the pressure was becoming a little overwhelming. "Our town can use all the help it can get, between the natural disasters and the recent murders. We don't need any more setbacks, and I appreciate all you're doing to help bring new people in."

"We've gotten a few calls for residential inquiries as well as businesses looking for properties to expand, since the Spring Festival," Tia responded. "I think the Food, Wine, and Art Festival will bring in the most."

"Speaking of that, did you get my deposit for the gala venue?"

"Yes, I did. Thank you. I emailed you a receipt, so check your inbox when you get back to your office. Let me know if you don't get it."

"I will."

"Will there even *be* a gala without the art auction?" Calvin asked.

"There *has* to be an auction. The town depends on it." Laura rubbed her temples. "David is contacting some people he knows who owe him a few favors."

"I'll make some calls as well." Dijon watched as David and his team left the restaurant. "Garcia isn't the only one with connections."

"That would be fantastic." Laura smiled. "Thank you all so much." She glanced at her watch again and groaned. Tommy wasn't going to be happy with her if she was late for something else again. "I really must run. I look forward to hearing from you soon." She waved and made her way outside to the marina parking lot, and then stopped short. What else could possibly go wrong?

Derks, Bryce, and Miley were waiting by her car.

She held up her hands before they could speak. "I'm sorry, but you're going to have to make an appointment if you want to speak with me."

Her work/life balance hadn't been so great lately, and her husband was at his wits' end with her. She understood completely, and would be frustrated with him if the tables were turned. She loved her job as mayor, but now that her daughters were getting older, their schedules were busier. It was hard to juggle being a wife, mother, and the mayor, and do a good job at all of them. She needed an assistant, but the town's budget couldn't afford that until it got back on its feet.

This last festival needed to pay off in a big way, and that started with the art.

"Just give me five minutes," Derks said.

Laura stepped around him and unlocked her car. "I don't have five minutes, Mr. Calloway. I wish I did. I could use five minutes myself. I truly am sorry." She climbed into her car and closed the door, swearing she heard the words "*you will be*" as she drove away.

Looking in her rear-view mirror as she left the marina, she watched the coaches in a heated argument with each other and wondered what that was all about.

* * *

"Wow, and he cooks, too." Olivia watched Hank work his magic at her stove, wearing a pair of gray FBI sweatpants and a dark blue, form-fitting t-shirt that matched his eyes.

He looked over his shoulder and winked. "Someone has to feed us, and I've experienced your cooking." He shot her a horrified look. "No offense."

The smells of homemade spaghetti sauce and meatballs had her mouth watering and stomach growling. "No offense taken. I've experienced my cooking, too." She laughed. "Take-out was my best friend during medical school."

"Growing up, my mom made us all take turns cooking."

"Us all?"

"My younger brother, sister, stepfather, mother, and myself. We each had to pick a night to cook. Then on the weekends we ordered take out on one night and went out to eat on the other."

"Smart woman." Olivia set the table while Hank talked.

"The experience set me up well for being on my own." He smiled as he sliced the Italian bread, put it in a basket, and brought it to the table.

"That's so nice you have those memories." She filled water glasses and poured red wine into two wine glasses.

"Yeah, it is." His eyes filled with fondness as he carried the bowl of sauce and meatballs over to the table.

Olivia grabbed the bowl of pasta and carried that over, then they both sat down to dish out their plates and eat in silence. She took a moment to moan as basil, oregano, and garlic pepper burst over her tastebuds, mixing with fresh parmesan cheese.

"Thank your mother for me."

He laughed. "Done."

"Do you get to see your family very often now that you're not in Florida?" She took a sip of her cabernet sauvignon.

"Not as much as I'd like to. They're retired and are traveling a lot these days. I try to get home for the holidays when I can."

The holidays were the hardest for her. Having no one to spend them with could be so lonely. "What about your brother and sister?"

His face dimmed a little before he took a sip of wine. "My sister passed away, and my brother moved to California."

Olivia dropped her fork. "I am so sorry."

"It's okay. It was a long time ago." Hank shrugged. "My mother had me with her first husband. After my father passed away, my mom married my stepfather. He had my brother with his first wife, and then together they had my sister. We were all really close, so her unexpected passing was hard on everyone. My parents dealt with it by retiring and traveling the world. My brother moved across the country. And, well, I threw myself into my work."

"We all have our own ways of healing from tragedy. When my parents died, I focused on college and later med school. So, I get it. Believe me. Keeping busy is a great way to forget about your troubles. It's the quiet moments alone that are hard to bear."

His gaze met hers and he hesitated like he wanted to say something, then he smiled softly. "Thank you."

"You're welcome," she replied just as softly. "I know I protested in needing your protection now that we know the real Cattleman Killer is back, but I have to say, I'm glad you're here. I don't like being alone, either."

A horrible screech sounded from outside.

Hank surged to his feet and grabbed his gun. "Stay here."

"No way." Olivia scrambled after him.

She wore yoga pants, a t-shirt, and bare feet. Not chancing being left behind, she slipped her toes into a pair of flip flops and followed Hank outside, keeping close behind him. He methodically did a sweep around her cottage, by the water, along the edge of the trees, and out front by their vehicles. When he was sure there wasn't anything out there, he slipped his gun into the waistband of his sweatpants.

"That noise sounded horrible. What do you think it was?" Olivia asked him as they approached her front door.

His eyes never stopped moving, scanning his surroundings, assessing, watching. "Most likely a wild animal."

"Poor thing." Olivia couldn't help but do the same. "That sounded painful."

"Unfortunately, in this neck of the woods, it's all about survival of the fittest." He opened the door to her cottage.

She followed him inside and locked the door behind them, checking it twice.

"That was enough excitement for one evening, thank you very much. You cooked, so I clean up. That was *my* mother's rule growing up." Olivia started clearing the table.

Hank went out to the living room to turn on the evening news.

"Help yourself to more wine," she added. "I'll be done in a few minutes."

"Thanks," he said and did so while she filled the dishwasher.

"I might not be able to cook, but I'm a great baker. I baked a cake earlier today. Would you like a piece?"

"I haven't had cake in years. That sounds delicious."

She lifted the floral plastic cake topper off the platter her mother had given her, then dropped it on the floor as she screamed.

Hank came flying into the kitchen with wine spilled all over his shirt. "What's wrong?" He searched her eyes.

She couldn't get the words out as she made it to the trash in time to vomit and then pointed to the counter. Hank's gaze followed the direction of her hand, and he flinched while letting out a curse. Her cake was missing...

In its place lay a dead raccoon, branded with the letter D.

* * *

THE NEXT MORNING, Hank and Olivia sat in Trent's office, going over what had happened. They'd called the police the night before and Hank insisted she pack a bag and move in with him in the hotel. He didn't want to let her out of his sight after this latest event.

"These people are good," Hank said to Trent. "I think Olivia is right. There are a few of them. I was there last night. Someone had to be outside to draw us out of the cottage. Then someone slipped inside to leave their handiwork to mess with her head."

"I think it's a trio. Two men and one woman." Olivia still looked shook up from the night before. She twisted her hands together as she talked. "From all that I remember, and everything that has happened recently, that's my best guess."

"It could be the real killer or the copycat. We've been making strides on the first two murders thanks to your help, Olivia. This might be their warning for you

126

to back off. I want you staying with Hank until this whole mess is over with."

"Gladly." For once she didn't put up any arguments.

"If there are any clues at your place, we'll find them," Trent said. "In the meantime, just keep working on finalizing your autopsy report on Dr. Ali Lambert."

"Anything new on your old file for The Cattleman Killer?" The Sheriff turned his attention on Hank.

"I've gotten through the first three victims. Rebecca Fournier was a lawyer. Melanie Monroe was a stockbroker. Kristina Branch was a CFO. Nothing stands out to me as something that I missed."

"What about the fourth. The last woman to be murdered before Lilly... I mean, Olivia." The Sheriff checked his notes. "Cindy Williams. Wasn't she a doctor?"

"A pediatrician, yes. I haven't gotten to her file yet, but I will soon. In the meantime, don't worry about Olivia. I'll make sure nothing happens to her."

"See that you do. She's too important to this town, and a friend as well." Trent nodded at Olivia. "Not to mention my wife would kill me if one hair on her head is harmed."

"Copy that." It would kill Hank if anything happened to Olivia, but this might also be his only chance to draw The Cattleman Killer into the open. Hank didn't want to just catch the killer. Putting him behind bars wasn't good enough...

He would kill the bastard if it was the last thing he did.

"Okay, so if you don't need me anymore, I'm headed to the lab to get caught up on work." Oliva stood.

"Make sure you call me if you leave." Hank looked her in the eyes.

She nodded and left the room to walk down the hall to her office.

The Sheriff's phone rang.

"Sheriff West here." He listened for a minute, his eyes meeting Hanks. "We'll be right there, Laura. Just sit tight." He hung up, stood, and grabbed his hat.

"What's wrong?" Hank asked.

"Someone broke into the mayor's office and ransacked the place like they were looking for something. You up for a road trip?"

"Let's roll."

13

"ARE YOU OKAY, LAURA?" Stacy hugged her friend hard and didn't let go.

Trent, Hank, and the police had left an hour ago to work the case, and Stacy had shown up to lend her bestie some moral support. The mayor's office had been trashed; no spot left untouched. Filing cabinets were emptied, drawers pulled out and overturned, and the closet ransacked.

"I don't know what they were looking for. I certainly don't have any art here, and I don't keep any of the money the town makes on the premises. After all that your mother went through years ago, I am very careful to make sure I cover my ass."

"Maybe someone is trying to ruin the festival." Stacy let go of Laura.

"And I'll give you three guesses who that might be." Laura walked around the room. "I ran into the coaches last night. They wanted five minutes of my time, but I couldn't give it to them. Maybe this is their way of paying me back."

"I just don't understand why Derks is so desperate for money for new uniforms." Stacy sat on the edge of Laura's desk and tilted her head. "I remember his booster club holding several fund raisers earlier this year."

"Exactly!" Laura threw her hands up.

"I mean, I get that sports are expensive, but *come on.*"

"Or maybe the person who ransacked my office is part of that art theft ring Winston was talking about." Laura snapped her fingers, looking around the room. "Maybe they thought I kept some art in the office."

"Maybe, but Trent said Penelope's ex-boyfriend killed her in a crime of passion that had nothing to do with art." Stacy tried to remember everything her husband had told her as well as the notes she shared with Winston. "And Nolan suspected Fay left the door to the museum unlocked so the man she's having an affair with could come in after hours."

"It's obvious Nolan had a thing for Fay. Maybe he staged the art being stolen as a cover-up so people wouldn't suspect him of killing Fay out of jealousy over catching her and her lover together."

Stacy held up a finger. "Not to mention, Fay's death allowed Nolan to get the promotion he should have had over her in the first place."

"How convenient." Laura looked pensive.

"Or *Nolan* is her lover. I think Fay was playing with Nolan. Trent said Zoe found a love letter hidden in Fay's office. The letter was from Nolan to her, confessing his love. Fay kept it. If she wasn't interested, she would have thrown the letter out. I think she was stringing him along. Using him. And when he figured that out, he snapped."

"Or here's a thought." Laura raised an eyebrow. "Fay bit off more than she could chew. I think maybe she was having an affair with two men, and it came back to bite her in the butt. Men don't like to share."

"Speaking of men and sharing… how is it going with Tommy sharing time with *your* other love?"

"Ah, the old married-to-my-work issue." Laura sighed.

"Exactly. Trent and I have a good system going now, but I worry what will happen with us once the baby comes."

"It's not easy. At least your husband is the Sheriff, so he understands when big events happen that affect the town. My husband owns a car dealership. He has salesmen working for him, so he can leave whenever he wants to. I don't have that luxury right now. Once I can afford an assistant to help lighten my load, things will be better."

Stacy squeezed Laura's hand. "Just remember, kids grow up quickly. You can't do everything, Laura. Mom wouldn't expect you to. She missed out on a lot with me and my dad, but my dad was always there. I remember that. Your kids will remember who's there, too. You keep waiting for tomorrow, and today just might pass you by. You just have to learn to say *no* to a few things."

"I know. You're right." Laura inhaled a deep breath and let it out slowly. "Easier said than done."

"Amen to that, sister."

Laura's phone went off, indicating a text message. She checked the screen and blew out a sigh of relief. "David's contact came through."

"Thank the Lord." Stacy stood.

Laura fired off a response back and grabbed her purse. "Gotta run."

"To see a man about some art?" Stacy asked.

"No, to take my daughters and *my* man out to lunch." Laura winked and left without another word.

* * *

THE FOOD, Wine, and Art Festival was in full swing. The weekend consisted of tours of the historic district, wagon rides over covered bridges, with stops consisting of food-and-wine pairing samples, wine-and-cheese harbor cruises, and a parade. The town was filled with spectators, both locally and from out of town, with security ramped up. Everyone wore formal attire, adding an elegant flair to the event.

Olivia stood inside the Hamilton Barn with Stacy, Laura, and Tia. Zoe was working security with Trent and Hank, who were all dressed in formal attire as well, when she wasn't stealing glances at Jack. Remy was back at the harbor, manning the marina. Nolan was talking to Tia's brothers along with the Garcia crew. And Larry was adjusting the microphone.

Meanwhile, Winston and Lorelai were arguing over their camera crews' placement in covering the event. They pretended to hate each other, but genuine sparks were flying between them, and it was obvious to anyone who spent more than five minutes near the both of them.

"What a great venue for the gala and art auction." Olivia looked around the barn, impressed by what they had managed to pull off.

Garcia Events had decorated the high ceilings and rustic wood with twinkle lights and spring flowers everywhere. Tables with fancy tablecloths and gorgeous centerpieces were scattered about. Up front, there was a podium for the auctioneer. All around the room, amazing pieces of art were on display, waiting to be auctioned off.

"Garcia really came through with the art," Stacy said.

"Actually, my brother Dijon secured more than half of what you see here." Tia's voice filled with pride.

"Thanks to both of them, tonight won't be a bust," Laura said with relief.

"I just hope no one else gets hurt." Stacy's forehead creased with worry lines. "It seems like after every big event, a murder happens." She shivered. "It still terrifies me that a copycat killer is on the loose. That's why the press is still in town. I'm actually thankful. The more press in town, the more eyes looking around for anything suspicious. They're not going to leave until the killer is caught. I just wish it would happen, already." She placed a hand over her stomach and left it there.

"I have confidence your husband and Agent Masters will work together to bring this creep and his helpers to justice once and for all." Laura nodded. "You'll see."

No one knew the real Cattleman Killer had shown up, so now they had two killers on the loose. Hank had said serial killers thrived on getting away with murder. That they got off on the fame. So, he and the Sheriff had kept the killer's acts against Olivia a secret.

No one knew except the three of them.

If Winston or Lorelai got wind that she was Lilly Swanson, they wouldn't hesitate to announce it and get the scoop of the decade. So many times, Olivia wanted to confide in her friends, but she just couldn't risk it. The more she stayed out of the news, the more desperate the killer would become. Eventually he had to make a mistake.

And when he did, she would be there waiting.

She'd decided she couldn't live in fear anymore. Couldn't keep running. It was time she took back her power. She ran her hand down the chain around her neck and wrapped her fingers around the cross with her parents' names on it. She could do this. She wasn't the same scared, helpless young woman she had been five years ago.

And she wasn't alone.

"Hey, you okay?" Hank whispered in her ear as he came up beside her to check in, lightly bumping her shoulder with his.

"I'm better now." Olivia smiled up at him.

He never failed to take her breath away with his movie-star golden-blond looks, rich blue eyes, and sexy dimples. Living with him had been easy, natural... and that was scary. They had only made love the one time, both keeping a respectable distance yet growing closer with every conversation.

Olivia knew why *she* was keeping her distance. She was afraid of letting him in completely, only to be hurt when this case was solved and he left. But she couldn't quite figure out why *he* was keeping his distance. He claimed to need to stay alert, but she could tell there was more to it than that.

She still felt he was hiding something from her.

Until he trusted her enough to let her in, they could never truly be more than just friends. Intimacy would only complicate things, but she had to admit, he had become her *best* friend. She knew he would be there for her if she needed him for anything.

"You left your hair down." He studied her in her body-hugging, strapless, red, floor-length gown that Tia had insisted she wear, then he gave her a lopsided grin. "I like it. Your hair, I mean. It suits you."

"It's a lot longer than it used to be. It sounds silly, I know, but I like how it wraps around me. I feel protected, like it's my armor. And honestly, I thought it would help disguise me. Obviously, that didn't work. I should probably cut it."

"Don't," he said a little too quickly. "You look beautiful." He cleared his throat. "Objectively speaking."

She smiled fully. "Well, thank you." She took in his tailored-to-perfection, Navy-blue tuxedo that showcased his muscles beneath. "You clean up pretty well yourself, there, Masters. Very gallant."

He held out his arm. "Care to join me in a dance?"

"Why, I thought you'd never ask." She took his arm and followed him to the dance floor, where a band played on the stage to entertain the guests until the auction started.

Tommy and Laura danced, looking happier than Olivia had seen them since she'd met them. Stacy had told her about Laura's lunch date with her family. Must be it did the trick. Stacy and Trent held each other close, swaying to the music. Zoe and Jack looked thoroughly besotted with each other. Even Winston had asked Lorelai to dance, and she'd said *yes*, surprising only him, apparently.

The rest of the evening went by in a blur, and for the first time in a while, Olivia felt safe. Coldwater Cove was becoming her home. They were sitting at a table, watching people bid until the last piece of art was sold. People were starting to leave, when suddenly Winston and Lorelai walked quickly over to their table.

"Can we talk in private?" Winston asked Stacy.

Trent frowned. "Whatever you have to say, you can say it in front of all of us."

Winston ignored Trent and looked at Stacy. "It's your call."

"The media and law enforcement don't always see eye-to-eye," she explained to the rest of them. "Given I married and am having this sheriff's baby, I think I can make an exception this time." She laughed. "Go ahead."

"I had my suspicions, and so did Lorelai," Winston said.

Stacy arched a brow. "Since when did you two start working together?"

He shrugged, his face flushing slightly. "Like you

said. The more heads the better, if we want to catch this copycat killer."

"If we work together to cover the story, then both our networks get the scoop," Lorelai added. "A little DNA and one savvy source later, we've got a new lead."

"And what exactly is the lead?" Trent asked.

"David Garcia isn't really David Garcia." Winston's eyes filled with excitement.

"Then who is he?" Laura looked shell shocked.

"David Perez," Lorelai said. "He changed his name several years ago."

"Why would he change his last name?" Stacy asked.

"David Perez used to work for another event planner years ago, but he was fired after being arrested for assault." Winston shook his head. "He slept with the wrong powerful man's wife while on the job. He claimed self-defense and was acquitted, but he had to change his last name and start over."

"I thought I recognized him, and I remembered that story, so I told Winston," Lorelai said. "Winston managed to get his DNA off a glass from The Claw, and I had a source that verified his identity."

"What does this mean?" Olivia asked.

"Garcia is a ladies' man and has a track record for assault. He worked closely with the museum on purchasing the art for the festival, and he stepped in front of Fay during her argument with the Little League coaches," Hank speculated, his gaze scanning everyone at their table. "I think we just found the person Fay Allenby was having an affair with."

Laura stood, her face livid.

"Where are you going?" Trent asked.

"To do what I should have done a while ago." She marched off in David's direction with an angry gait.

Everyone at the table scrambled to their feet to follow.

"Just the person I wanted to see." David smiled at Laura. "I would say the auction was a huge success."

"But at what price?" She clenched her fists.

"I'm afraid I don't know what you're talking about?" He stepped back, scanning them all warily.

"I don't even know who you are, David *Perez*. You assaulted a woman? How could you?"

His face paled. "I didn't assault a woman. Her husband assaulted me, and I defended myself. A jury voted me not guilty."

"You had an affair with a married woman. It's no wonder her husband assaulted you. I don't care that the jury voted you innocent. You lied to me, and to everyone. You're a fraud. How many other women's lives have you ruined since then? What about poor Fay?"

"You slept with Fay?" Nolan asked, his face growing hard.

"She seduced him," Hannah clarified, stepping in front of David.

David squeezed her arm and then pulled her back. "I saw your little love note." He gave Nolan a pathetic look. "Fay felt sorry for you and didn't have the heart to shoot you down, but she wasn't into you, man. I can't help it the ladies adore me."

"I never would have hired you if I had known," Laura interjected. "And you can bet I'll make sure no one else on the East Coast does, either."

"You ungrateful bitch," David hissed.

Jude grabbed David's arm.

Hank stepped in front of Laura.

"Easy, there, Garcia or Perez or whatever the hell your name is," Trent said in a deadly voice. "You harm one hair on the mayor's head, I'll throw you in jail and not think twice about it. Not to mention, her husband is twice your size and a former football player. Messing with her would not be a wise decision."

David shrugged off Jude's hand and glared at the Sheriff. "I already did my time. You can't prove I did anything wrong here. Sex isn't a crime, last time I checked."

"No, but murder is," Trent said. "You have a record. It wouldn't surprise me if you were involved in the art theft smuggling ring happening up and down the coast. You have the perfect cover and access as an event planner."

"You're crazy."

"And you're a person of interest. Don't plan on leaving town anytime soon."

With one last look of outrage, David and his assistants left the venue, creating a flurry of gasps and horrified stares.

14

"I CAN'T BELIEVE you talked me into this." Zoe clutched the rail of Jack's sailboat the next evening.

He'd met a group of tourists at the Food, Wine, and Art Festival, and had promised them a sunset wine-and-cheese sail. The only reason she'd gone with him was because he couldn't manage the sailing as well as serving the wine and cheese by himself.

That didn't mean she wasn't scared to death.

"Nothing is going to go wrong, Zoe." Jack patted her shoulder. "I'm just thankful for your help."

"Sheriff West gave me the night off and ordered me to take a break. But I heard David and his team disappeared."

"You're kidding. Isn't he a person of interest in Fay's murder?"

"He sure is, but no one has seen him, Hannah, or Jude since they stormed out of the festival last night."

"Why would he run if he's not guilty?"

"He swears he wasn't the one to kill Fay. And now that his identity is exposed, his career is ruined. Men like him don't handle being bested very well. I'm sure he'll start over with yet another new identity someplace else. Agent Masters put in a call to his colleagues to be on the lookout for all of them."

"I hope they get caught, but I have to say I'm kind of relieved they're gone."

"Same here."

They sailed along the coast, with Jack pointing out landmarks, wildlife, and famous lighthouses. Zoe served the guests with plates of assorted cheeses paired with various samples of wine until they'd had their fill. The sunset was gorgeous, with orange, pink, and purple lighting up the sky. Zoe forgot how much she missed the water and being on a boat. She closed her eyes and inhaled the salty sea air. Gulls squawked overhead and waves lapped against the boat.

Opening her eyes, a movement to her right caught her attention. She squinted at the shoreline. They had gone farther north than normal. She thought she saw something dart into the woods. In fact, it had looked like a couple of shadows. She frowned.

"Did you see anything along the shore over there." She pointed.

"No, why?"

"I could have sworn I saw a couple of people dart into the woods."

"There's nothing out here but woods. Maybe it was a bear and her cubs. Or a moose and her calf."

"Maybe, but my gut is telling me it's something else. I'm making a note to check it out when we reach the marina."

"I'll go with you. It's pretty remote out there and will be fully dark by the time you get there by car. We still have a killer on the loose."

"But you're not an officer of the law."

"I'm pretty much everything else. Firefighter, Snowplow Guy, Bartender, Pub Owner. I think I can handle it. Besides, it will be easier to get to by boat."

"Okay, but you take your orders from me."

"Yes, ma'am." He saluted her.

"Are you worried about me, Captain?" A soft smile tipped up the corners of her lips. They hadn't talked about where they stood since making love, but they had been spending a lot more time together. That was enough for her right now.

"Always." He tweaked her nose and winked.

Her heart skipped a beat. Maybe she was ready for more after all.

It wasn't long before they reached the marina and dropped their guests off.

"You headed back out, Jack?" Remy asked from the dock.

"Yeah, why?"

"There's a chance for a thunderstorm in a little while."

"We have some business to check on up the coast," Zoe said. "Possibly some lost hikers in a pretty remote area on the shoreline."

"Or possibly just some wildlife," Jack added, his voice filled with skepticism.

"Better safe than sorry," Zoe said. "I'll radio the Sheriff if we find anything."

"Roger that." Remy nodded. "The Coast Guard is further down the coast, so they won't be available to help if you need them."

"No worries. I know what to do."

The gorgeous sunset faded away as Jack sailed out of the harbor. It wasn't long before clouds rolled in, and raindrops started to sprinkle. The evening air brought a chill with it. Zoe had her firearm with her like she always did, even though she was out of uniform. All she wanted to do was make sure no one was in trouble.

"This is the spot." Jack pulled the boat close to shore.

This far north, the water was deep enough for boats to come right up to the shoreline. Zoe stood on the edge of the sailboat and leapt to the shore.

"Hey, you didn't say anything about going ashore," Jack hollered after her. "I can't leave the boat unattended."

"I'll be fine. I have my piece. I won't be long." She looked at his worried expression. "Everything will be okay, Jack."

"Well, just note that I don't like this."

"Noted." She saluted him and then turned around to investigate.

Scanning the ground, she didn't see any animal prints. But she did see a couple sets of footprints. "This is the Sheriff's department. Is anyone out there?" Her hand hovered over her weapon.

No answer.

A crack of thunder sounded overhead.

"Call out if you need help." She paused a beat.

Still no answer.

It started raining now.

"Zoe, come on. The weather is taking a turn for the worse. We need to get out of here." Jack's voice sounded urgent.

"Coming," Zoe hollered, and started to make her way back.

She spotted a tarp near the shore. What the heck was that doing out in the middle of the woods? There weren't any trails that led here and no roads for a car. Someone had to hike this way. What could they possibly be storing? Making her way over to the bundle, she lifted the edge and gasped.

The missing art from the museum.

It was wrapped in protective casing and stored beneath the tarp. Flipping the tarp over, she placed the art in the middle and wrapped the tarp around the load.

Holding the end, she dragged the load to the edge of the coast.

She knew from her days with the Coast Guard that they couldn't patrol the whole coast at once. With the water being so deep right here, boats from Canada and Nova Scotia could bypass customs by not going into the harbor. They would pull right up to the edge like Jack had done, and smuggle goods out of the country undetected.

"What on earth did you find?" Jack asked.

"The missing art and a few sets of footprints, but no one was there. I wasn't going to leave the art there and risk the thieves coming back for it later. This might be our only chance to retrieve it. Are you good with your hands?"

"You tell me." He winked.

She rolled her eyes. "Then you should have no problem catching these."

His face paled. "Thank you for the vote of confidence, but those are expensive. What if we lose one?"

"Not too long ago, we thought we lost them all. Salvaging some is better than none in my book."

"And what if the smugglers come back?" He frowned. "Those aren't people you want to mess with."

"It's part of the job, Jack. Now get ready." She unwrapped the tarp and started tossing him piece by piece until they had all the art on board just as a streak of lightning zipped across the sky.

"Hurry up and get on this boat so I know you're safe. You're making me nervous." A muscle in his jaw bulged.

She smiled a little, his words warming her heart, then she ran a few steps and jumped. A wave pushed the boat out further, and she landed hard against the side, clutching the edge as she grunted in pain.

"Shit!" Her hands were slipping. The rain was coming down harder, making the wet fiberglass slick.

"Hold on!" Jack pulled the boat away from shore a bit and then snagged her arm and yanked hard just as her hands gave way.

She rolled across the floor in an unceremonious heap, breathing hard. She pulled herself up to her feet and joined him at the helm when shots rang out. They both ducked. She spun around, drawing her weapon and taking aim at the shore. Another shot rang out just missing her head. She dove for cover.

Whoever was shooting at them was hiding. Jack gunned the engine, and they picked up speed, getting underway. They were almost out of range when the third shot rang out. The boat started taking on water.

"Mayday mayday," Jack said into his radio.

"Do you think we can make it back to the harbor?"

"I'm hoping so, but those waves are getting bigger than I like."

No sooner did he say that when a massive wave hit the boat and it capsized. Everything happened in a blur. Zoe's training kicked in, and she managed to get the life raft and its container free from the railing. She threw it into the water and pulled the rip cord. The buoyancy chambers of the life raft automatically filled with air.

Jack grabbed the art and managed to get that on board. Silent and focused on their roles, they both climbed inside and cut the cord from the sailboat just in time before it sank. The life raft had a cover so they would stay dry.

Zoe checked the inventory on board. They had a water scoop, sponge, emergency paddle, first aid kit, and a waterproof bag of various other emergency provisions. She closed her eyes, her heart pounding as she remembered what it was like the day she had lost her fiancé.

She never should have gotten on a boat again.

"Hey, I know what you're thinking." Jack reached out and took her hand.

She opened her eyes and blinked back tears, unable to speak past the lump in her throat.

"This situation wasn't like before. You did great. We recovered the stolen art from the museum, and you got us on the life raft."

"You lost your boat because of me," she managed to say.

"Not because of you. Because of criminals who need to be put away. You did your job and stopped them from smuggling the art. That's going to go a long way in helping Coldwater Cove get back on its feet. Don't worry about my boat. That's what insurance is for."

"You could have died."

"So could you, but we didn't."

"I don't know what I would have done if I lost you." A little sob slipped out. "I-I can't go through that again."

He scooted closer and pulled her onto his lap, wrapping his arms around her as the powerful waves tossed them around. "I've learned you can't go through life with what-ifs. That's not living, Zoe. I haven't wanted to open up or share my life with anyone until I met you."

"But I don't know if I can give you what you deserve."

"Don't put pressure on yourself. Let's just take this day by day and see what happens. All I know is I can't live without you, and I'll take that in any form you can give."

"Okay."

"Yeah?"

She nodded and kissed him on the mouth, deciding

to take his advice and stop thinking about what ifs. All she knew was that he was worth the risk. Whatever that looked like.

* * *

"I GAVE you the day off, Zoe. What the hell happened?" Trent sat across from his deputy and Jack in Remy's office in the harbor.

Zoe wrapped the blanket Remy had given her tighter around herself. "Jack and I took some tourists on a wine-and-cheese cruise."

"We headed north for a change and further inland than I normally go," Jack added, drying his hair with a towel Remy had given him.

"I spotted something on the shoreline," Zoe continued. "Jack thought maybe it was an animal, but my gut was telling me it wasn't. With a killer on the loose, I was worried it was some lost hikers or someone in trouble.

"Remy said you dropped the tourists off, so why would you go back without calling for backup?" Trent frowned at her. He didn't like his officers putting themselves in unnecessary danger.

"I normally would have, but I didn't want to risk losing our window of opportunity. Besides, I had Jack with me."

Trent shook his head. "No offense, Jack, but you're not a cop."

Jack shrugged. "None taken, but I wasn't about to let Zoe go it alone."

Trent nodded. "I appreciate that."

"Anyway," Zoe interjected. "I wasn't surprised when I saw human footprints. I knew my hunch was right, I just didn't know if I would encounter friend or foe."

"I'm glad you carried your piece on you." Trent took his hat off and ran a hand over his buzzed head.

"Always."

"I have a concealed-carry as well, and had my gun on the boat. You never know when you might encounter a crazy tourist," Jack pointed out.

Remy grunted. "You aren't kidding. The things I've had to deal with since taking over for Charley Wentworth would shock you. People are downright crazy."

"They sure are," Zoe said. "I was completely surprised when I found the missing art in a tarp by the shore. I know the issues we had over being able to police the vast shoreline when I was in the Coast Guard. The water is so deep, it's impossible to catch every smuggler."

"Especially with boats not having to come into the marina," Remy added. "There's no way to make them go through customs unless they're caught by the Coast Guard. We see smuggling happen way too often."

"Did you get a look at the person who shot at you?" Trent asked Zoe.

"No, I couldn't see a thing."

"So, you have no way of knowing if it was more than one person?"

She shook her head. "I saw more than one set of tracks, but when the shots rang out, I couldn't tell if they came in more than one direction."

"The bullets didn't hit anything on my boat that I remember, but it sank anyway, so there's no way of knowing what kind of gun they came from," Jack said.

"Sorry about your boat. I'll have some divers see if they can find anything." Trent made a note. "I'm just glad that I checked in with Remy because of the storm. I had no idea you two went out again. You're lucky you didn't go down with the boat."

"I'm not worried about my sailboat. That's what I

have insurance for. If it wasn't for Zoe's rescue skills, we might have gone down with the boat for sure," Jack said with pride and awe. "I've never seen someone so efficient with a life raft, rescue equipment, and knowing when to cut the tether free."

"It's just part of the job." Zoe shrugged, clearly uncomfortable with compliments. "I'm glad you salvaged the art."

"What will happen now?" Remy asked. "Will the art go back to the museum?"

"The art was purchased by the mayor's office and donated by the museum for the auction, so it still belongs to the town. Maybe Nolan can store it until the next auction. I'll let Mayor Flemming make that call." Trent narrowed his eyes. "Then we try to find our thief or thieves and throw the book at them."

"Do you think it was Garcia and his crew?" Zoe asked.

"Could be." Trent rubbed his jaw. "No one has seen or heard from them since the auction, even though I told him not to skip town."

"Hiding out in the woods and trying to smuggle the art for some cash would be a great way to start over," Jack said.

"Well, Agent Masters has some feelers out. Garcia can't hide forever," Trent said. "In the meantime, why don't you two go get dry and get some rest. It's late."

"That sounds great to me." Zoe shivered.

"You hungry?" Jack asked.

"Starving, but nothing's open," Zoe said.

"Lucky for you, I know a place." Jack laughed. "I'll take you home after," Jack added, with eyes only for Zoe.

Trent looked at them both curiously. Something had definitely changed between them. "Don't even think of showing your face at work tomorrow,

Granger." Trent pointed a finger at her. "That's an order."

"Don't worry, Sheriff, I'll keep her out of trouble." Jack grinned.

"Something tells me you're no better at staying out of trouble than she is. I have enough things to worry about." Trent clenched his jaw. "Like catching a killer."

15

"THIS IS A GAME CHANGER." Laura couldn't believe the art had been recovered. If she could hold a second auction as a fundraiser, maybe she could finally help the Little League coaches. After all, the kids shouldn't have to suffer because their coach was insane.

"I agree," Stacy said. "That girl pitcher, Rosy, really is incredible. I think she stands a good chance of helping the team win the World Series. If that happens, then that will definitely help put Coldwater Cove on the map."

"What do you have in mind?" Zoe asked. "Trent won't let me come in to work today, but I can't just sit around and do nothing. I hate when it rains. It makes everything so gloomy." The lights flickered in the diner. "If the power goes out, I'll lose my mind."

The women were having lunch at The Lost Horizon, which had become the norm as of late. Jack had stopped in to drop off flour to Betty Ford because her shipment had been delayed. Even though they were both restaurant owners, their establishments were known for different things. She made the best diner food, and he made the best pub food. The most important thing was they were Coldwater Covians, and that meant supporting each other.

He kept looking over at Zoe like a love-struck puppy dog, and Zoe kept stealing glances at him as well. It was obvious to everyone that the traumatic event they had just gone through had bonded them even closer than they had already been. Lately, wherever one was, the other wasn't far behind.

"I'm sure you could think of something to do with a certain pub owner if the power goes out." Laura winked.

"So, back to planning the auction." Zoe blushed.

"The barn is rented out until summer, but I can see if my brothers know of any other places to hold another auction," Tia said, bringing Laura's thoughts back to the conversation at hand.

"That would be great." Laura made a note in her notebook.

"We're here to help if you need anything else. It must be hard to plan everything with David Garcia gone." Olivia shuddered. "Not that I mind. The man gave me the creeps."

"No kidding." Laura frowned. "He was a little obsessed with you, more so than any of the other women he seduced. I think it's because you were unattainable. It was clear he didn't like to hear *no*."

"There was something about him that made me think it had to do with more than that." Olivia shrugged. "I don't know why. The way he looked at me so intensely. It was unnerving, for sure."

"Well, we don't have to worry about him now." Zoe nodded once, firmly.

"Or do we?" Stacy raised an eyebrow at them. "Trent suspects he might be hiding out in the woods. We need to have that art auction as soon as possible. I think Garcia-slash-Perez was counting on that money as his ticket out of here. He's not going to give up that easily on getting the art back."

"You're right," Laura agreed. "David's dangerous. We need a plan before he can cause any more damage."

"Why don't we save time and money and just have the auction at the community center?" Olivia looked at Laura.

"I think you're onto something." Laura made another note. "I'll see when the center is free and get something on the books right away. And I'll have Nolan store the art in the museum again. Now that all the locks have been changed and the security cameras updated, keeping it safe shouldn't be a problem."

"I'll talk to Jack about donating some food," Zoe said.

"I'm sure Betty would be more than happy to donate some food from The Lost Horizon as well," Olivia offered.

"Larry knows a DJ who might provide music for the entertainment," Laura added. "It's worth a shot to see if he's available."

"And I can talk to the coaches about organizing a time that works for them." Stacy looked at the group. "I'm covering their plans for the World Series anyway, and I'm sure they'll be thrilled with the idea of new uniforms and a sendoff we can present them with before the big game."

"Sounds like a plan. Then maybe *finally* I can be done with the craziness my life has become, and get back to a normal schedule before the summer festivals start." Laura sighed, ready for spring to be over. This season hadn't been about life and rebirth. It had been about death and murder. She wasn't sure how much more Coldwater Cove could take.

Lightning lit up the sky and a loud boom of thunder sounded ominously behind.

***

I stood in the shadows of the woods with the hood to my raincoat up, watching as the mayor and her groupies walked out of The Lost Horizon. Squinting through the rain, I focused my attention on one woman only.

Dr. Olivia Jones.

She would always be Lilly Swanson to me. Anger began to churn deep within my gut. It was all because of Special Agent Hank Masters that I wasn't able to get to Lilly. He hadn't let her out of his sight since I'd broken into her car. He'd even gone so far as to have her move in with him in his hotel room. That complicated things, making it more difficult to stalk her.

I thrive on complicated.

I rubbed my hands together, knowing I was damn good. I'd stumped him five years ago, and I was besting him now. They weren't any closer to catching me. That filled me with pride, but my smile soon turned to a scowl. It irritated me the cops were keeping her identity a secret and hadn't revealed that the real Cattleman Killer had arrived.

I'd be damned if I would keep letting the copycat steal my thunder.

Lilly walked to her car beneath her umbrella. She waved to the others, and then glanced around with a wide-eyed look as if she sensed me. I ducked back behind a tree, my arousal stirring. She felt the connection between us the same that I did. I knew it in my gut.

She frowned and then climbed into her car.

"That's right, princess. I'm coming for you." Here was my chance to grab her. Then everyone would know the truth.

"I can't believe how reckless you're being. What are you doing out here?" he hissed in my ear.

"Now more than ever we need to lay low," she whispered. "You of all people should know that."

I rolled my eyes. "I don't have time for this, you two." I'd picked the lock of a random car in the back of the parking lot in anticipation of this very moment. I placed a text from a stolen phone I had, setting my plan in motion. Climbing into the vehicle, I hotwired it. Of course, they stayed with me. I planned to ditch the car when I was finished with her, and then I would leave town with no one the wiser.

I was unstoppable.

"We were so close to getting everything we wanted," he said, "but you keep messing things up."

"Why can't you just trust us for once?" she added, her frustration clearly evident in her whiney tone.

"I did trust you and look at what happened. I didn't mess up, *you* both did. Your so-called plan didn't work," I spat and pulled out behind Lilly, following her at a safe distance. Close enough not to lose her, but far enough away not to be seen. "I'm through with playing these games."

"Give us a little more time," he said. "Have patience."

"My patience has reached its limit. I'm through with watching and waiting," I growled. "This time, we're doing things *my* way. Because my way always works."

"What are you planning to do?" she asked, her voice filled with worry.

"I'm getting back what's mine and finishing what I started."

* * *

OLIVIA PULLED out of The Lost Horizon parking lot and turned her windshield wipers on high. The rain was coming down in buckets now. She gripped the steering wheel and focused on the road heading out of town.

She'd had the oddest feeling that someone was watching her when she was in the parking lot, but she chalked it up to being paranoid. As soon as she'd ducked out of the rain and into her car, she'd gotten a text. The message said that Sheriff West wanted her to meet him at the old abandoned lighthouse up the coast. That there had been a break in the case, and he needed her expertise.

The caller ID came up Coldwater Cove Sheriff's Department, so she didn't think twice about responding to it. She tried to shoot Hank a text, but the storm was making the cell reception spotty the further she drove out of town. She was supposed to meet him after lunch back at her office, but he would most likely be with Trent anyway. She always carried her medical bag with her in case an emergency like this happened.

She prayed they hadn't found another dead body.

Navigating the winding road that led to the coast, she finally turned onto the road that snaked along a cliff and headed north. The sky grew darker, the thunder and lightning more prevalent, as the rain fell in sheets now. There wasn't much of a shoulder, and only a small guard rail, setting her nerves on edge.

She'd never been to this lighthouse, but she'd heard about it. It was one of the oldest lighthouses and a historical landmark. The structure had been condemned, so no one was allowed inside. It sat on the edge of a cliff, allowing most people to admire its charm from boat cruises rather than on the treacherous road that led to it.

It couldn't be much farther. She glanced at the navigation system in her car, but then headlights in her rear-view mirror blinded her. Jerking the wheel, she barely maintained control as she whipped the mirror up. It was raining too hard, and the sky was dark with storm clouds, so it was impossible to see who followed her.

Squinting, she could just make out the lighthouse ahead in the distance, and relief filled her. Maybe it was someone from the Sheriff's office who followed her. Then again, why didn't they have their police lights on? The car sped up and tapped her bumper. She jerked forward, and her heart slammed against her chest.

This was no cop who followed her.

If only she could get to the lighthouse, the Sheriff would be there, Hank would be there, and she would be safe. The car tapped her bumper harder this time. Her breathing grew choppy, and she had to struggle not to hyperventilate. She sped up and pulled into the light-house parking lot, and her heart bottomed out.

It was empty.

She'd been played. Swallowing past her dry throat, she swung her car around toward the entrance. A car faced her head-on, it's headlights on high beam, blinding her. Everything in her gut told her it was *him*. She couldn't let him catch her.

He would kill her for sure this time.

Gunning the engine with all that she had, she charged him and faked to the right. When he fell for it, she surged around him to the left, fishtailing until she hit the road, then straightened her car out with him hot on her tail. She could tell by his driving he was furious.

This time when he hit her, he didn't hold back. She felt the impact crunch the back of her bumper. Her head whipped forward, her seatbelt locking, then her head whipped back with a crack. She cried out in pain, sobbing as she thought of never having told Hank how she really felt about him.

His face flashed before her mind as her car spun in a three-sixty. She saw a truck's headlights coming her way from the opposite direction way off in the distance, but that's the last thing she saw before she broke through the guard rail.

Everything happened in slow motion.

Her car flipped over and over, the world around her spinning wildly, making her dizzy. Just when she thought she was going to get sick, her car came to a crashing stop on its hood at the base of the cliff. She hung upside down in agony with water touching the top of her head. She lay that way for a while, feeling the blood rush to her head.

She heard footsteps crunching gravel just before her world went black.

* * *

HANK KNOCKED on Sheriff West's office door. He was supposed to meet Olivia in her office when she finished lunch with the girls. He was early, so he thought this would be the perfect time to discuss his theories on the murders with Trent.

Trent looked up and motioned him in, finishing a phone call. When he hung up, he shook his head. "How we can lose a work cell phone is beyond me. We don't have the budget to go around replacing new phones." He rubbed his temples and took off his hat. "Never mind that. What can I help you with?"

Hank carried his folder on The Cattleman Killer into the room and sat down across from the Sheriff. "I finished going through my old files."

"Anything new stand out to you?" Trent scrubbed a hand over his buzz cut. "Because I could use some good news right about now."

"Not really, but it did get me thinking. We've been looking for a man who did the killings and not having much luck in finding him." Hank gnawed the inside of his cheek, organizing his thoughts.

"Correct." Trent studied him with curiosity.

"Talking with Olivia got me thinking about how we've been approaching this investigation. She says when she was Lilly Swanson, she was sure there were three people who kidnapped her. One woman, and two men."

"That's true. Where are you going with this?"

"Larry said he heard more than one voice in the warehouse when Remy got jumped." Hank looked through his notes. "Nolan also claims he heard more than one voice when the art was stolen from the museum storage room."

"I think you're on to something." Trent nodded. "Deputy Granger also said she saw multiple footprints by the stolen art in the woods along the coast. There were three gunshots. Could have been from multiple people."

"Exactly." Hank flipped through more notes. "Maybe our real killer was pretending to be a copycat killer to throw everyone off. Maybe he has been involved in the art smuggling ring for the past five years, and that's why no one has seen or heard from him... until now."

Trent pointed at Hank. "You think seeing Lilly Swanson again pushed him over the edge, and he can't help coming out of hiding and revealing himself."

"It makes sense." Hank wrinkled his forehead as he drew circles on his notebook. "What do you think the branded D stands for?"

"A name possibly? I mean the guy brands his victims. People only brand something as proof that it belongs to them."

"Exactly. The sick bastard puts his stamp on them." Hank ground his teeth, finding it hard to remain objective when it came to The Cattleman Killer.

"I'm listening," Trent said. "What's your game plan?"

"I say we take a closer look at all our trios in town."

"Okay." Trent grabbed a piece of paper and pen and started writing. "Well, we have the Little League coaches: Derks, Bryce, and Miley."

"We also have the event planners: David, Jude, and Hannah," Hank pointed out. "If we can find them again, that is."

"I hate to say it," Trent winced as he wrote down more names, "but there's also the realtors: Dijon, Calvin, and Tia."

Hank paused for a moment, wrestling over his next words before adding, "Zoe also has two brothers: Dan and Scott."

Trent's face hardened. "Her credentials are impeccable. Besides, her brothers are estranged and they're not even in town."

"That we know of." Hank raised his hands. "Deputy Granger is new to town. We can't rule anyone out."

"You're new to town as well." Trent narrowed his eyes. "Didn't you say you had two siblings? A sister and a brother? What are their names?"

Hank felt a punch to the gut, but he'd opened this can of worms. He couldn't shy away from this conversation now. "Cynthia and Daryl, but mine aren't a possibility."

"I disagree. If you're suspecting Zoe, I think it's only fair we include everyone as a possibility, including you."

Hank put up his usual mask and said without emotion, "My sister is dead, and my brother is in rehab across the country."

The starch went out of Trent's stiff shoulders and rigid spine. "I'm sorry about that, man. I didn't know. No offense, but like you, I had to be sure."

"None taken, Sheriff." Hank tapped the paper before

them. "Notice the common denominator in all the trios?"

Trent looked at the list. "At least one of the male names in each group starts with the letter D."

"We find out which trio it is, and that is the name of our killer."

"Agreed."

"I want this guy caught more than anyone," Hank said, unable to control the deadly rage from vibrating his voice.

"Why is that?" Trent studied him carefully.

Hank opened his mouth to speak, but the Sheriff's cell phone rang, and Hank breathed out a sigh of relief. Trent answered, his face growing alarmed as he looked at Hank, and Hank's relief was short lived.

"I'm on my way." The Sheriff hung up and stood.

"What's wrong?" Hank surged to his feet.

"A truck driver on the north end of town just discovered a car that broke through the guardrails and rolled down the cliff by the old abandoned lighthouse."

Hank's gut tightened. "Anyone we know?"

"It's Olivia."

16

OLIVIA HEARD beeps as if from a machine, and she smelled the pungent odor of antiseptic. She opened her eyes to see Hank sleeping in a chair beside her. It was dark out, with only a soft light on by her bed. His clothes were wrinkled, his hair was a mess, and he needed a shave. He looked exhausted, yet so unbelievably perfect to her. She looked around the room and realized she was in the hospital. Touching her head, she winced. Her head ached something fierce.

"Liv? Oh, thank God, you're awake." Hank sat up and scooted closer to her bed, taking her hand in his. His deep blue gaze traced every inch of her face over and over, his expression a mix of worry and relief and something more she couldn't quite identify.

"What happened?" Her voice sounded hoarse.

"You don't remember?" He handed her a glass of water. "You've been in here for two whole days."

Her eyebrows shot up over that. She concentrated for a moment, and images started flooding back to her, making her nauseous. "I remember getting a text from the Sheriff's office, saying Trent wanted me to meet him at the old lighthouse up the coast. Something about a break in the case and needing my expertise."

"Trent said one of the phones from his office went missing."

The same sense of terrifying fear that she'd felt that day filled her once more. "I realized pretty quickly the message wasn't from his office when I showed up at the lighthouse and no one was there."

Hank frowned. "How did you end up driving over the cliff?"

"Someone followed me. Well, not just anyone." Her heart sped up as her gaze locked with his, and she inhaled a deep breath, exhaling before saying, "It was *him*."

Hank flinched and a muscle in his jaw hardened. "The Cattleman Killer? How do you know for sure?"

"He kept tapping my bumper, playing with me. I had to outsmart him in order to get around him. He was furious at being bested and ran me off a cliff. Just before I went over the edge, I saw a truck's lights off in the distance. I survived the fall but then moments before I blacked out, I heard footsteps. I thought for sure that was the end for me. That's all I remember. How did I get here?"

"That truck driver saved your life. If he hadn't been coming along when he did and stopped when he saw the broken guard rail, I don't think you would have made it. The Cattleman Killer never would have let you go willingly."

"I agree." She let out a sob.

He held her hand. "I know this is hard, but did you see his face or anyone else with him? Anything at all that might help us identify him?"

"No, it was raining so hard, and the sky was dark. I couldn't even make out the car or license plate. It all happened so fast." She rubbed her throbbing temples. "I'm sorry. I wish I could remember more."

"It's okay. Don't stress yourself. Maybe you'll remember more later." Concern filled his eyes, and tenderness laced his voice.

"All I could think about was that I would never see you again or get to tell you how I feel." Her voice hitched.

Hank closed his eyes briefly, then bent down and kissed her hand. "I can't even think about what I would have done if I lost you." His eyes opened and met hers, filling with the utmost sincerity as he said in barely more than a whisper, "I'm falling in love with you, Olivia Jones, and it scares the hell out of me."

Olivia sucked in a little breath and let out a happy cry. She never thought she would be happy to hear those words from anyone, but she was. He'd changed her life so completely. "I'm falling in love with you, too, Hank Masters, and I don't have a clue what to do about it." Tears streamed down her face.

"Awe, baby, don't cry." He wiped a tear away with his thumb, his own eyes filling with moisture as he bent down and kissed her lips softly. "We'll figure it out together, day by day. First things first, let's tell the doc you're awake. He said you have a concussion, but no broken bones. I'm just glad you remember me."

"You're pretty unforgettable." She cupped his cheek with her palm, and he turned his face in to kiss it.

"I'll be right back."

"Don't be gone long." She hated the tremor in her voice, but she couldn't help feeling uneasy, like this game of cat-and-mouse with the killer was far from over.

His gaze turned fierce and determined. "Oh, I'm not going anywhere without you from here on out. You can count on that. Just do me a favor."

"Anything."

"Remember how you feel about me right now, no matter what happens, and know I meant every word I said. Promise me, okay?" His face looked so intense, like this was very important to him.

"I promise," Olivia said, wanting nothing more than to put him at ease, yet a whisper snaked through her brain that there was more to Hank Masters than she knew about, and she just might not like what that was when she found out.

* * *

"THANKS FOR HAVING US ALL OVER," Olivia said to Stacy. "If I had to stay one more day inside Hank's hotel room, I would lose my mind. I haven't been cleared to go back to work yet, and he won't let me out of his sight unsupervised. I mean I get it... I just hate living like this. I feel like I'm on house arrest."

"You're very welcome. I love hosting girls' night, or in this case, lunch." Stacy beamed. "You said you wanted someplace private to talk, so I figured The Lost Horizon was out. The best part is, I didn't have to cook."

"That's the beauty of dating a restaurant owner." Zoe smiled as she unpacked the box of clam chowder, salad, bread, and dessert Jack had sent her with. "He spoils me."

"You two make such a cute couple." Laura set the table as Stacy poured the iced teas. "I'm happy for you both."

"Me, too," Tia said.

"Thanks, girls. Jack is pretty great." Zoe looked at Olivia and her face grew serious. "I know you don't like the extra security, Olivia, but you almost died. We still have a copycat killer on the loose, and like it or not, you fit the description of his victims. Dark hair, late twenties- early thirties, and successful."

"You have no idea," Olivia said just as seriously, and

they all looked at her with confusion. "That's what I wanted to talk to you ladies in private about." It was time. She needed to start trusting people, and who better than them?

"Well, you have my interest piqued." Stacy dug into her soup. "I'm all ears."

"I've never really had best friends. My parents died when I was in college, and I've been focused on my career ever since. I'm not very good with people."

"I think you've opened up so much since we first met you." Laura reached out and held Olivia's hand. "You're a part of our town now. One of us. That means something here in The Cove."

"Thank you. Coldwater Cove feels like home. I haven't been in a place that feels like home in a very long time."

"I know how you feel, Olivia." Tia took a sip of her iced tea. "As another outsider, you all have made me feel so welcome. That means more than you know."

"Same here," Zoe said. "After my fiancé died, I didn't think I would ever learn how to live again. Now look at me. A new boyfriend, some amazing friends, and I'm even back to boating. I couldn't have done any of that without you girls."

"I agree, but I don't trust easily." Olivia looked them each in the eye. "After I nearly died the other day, it made me realize life is too short not to share how you're feeling with the people who mean the most to you."

"Does this have to do with Hank?" Laura asked.

"Yes and no. We did tell each other we were falling in love with each other, but I don't know what that means for the future. He lives in Boston, and I plan to make tThe Cove my home, so we'll see, but I can't stress about that now. I asked you all here to talk about something other than Hank."

"Well, talk away," Stacy said. "The suspense is killing me."

"It's not that easy for me."

"Awe, honey, you can tell us anything," Tia said.

For the next hour, Olivia opened up about everything. She told them she used to live in Florida. She talked about her parents and how great life was. Then how life wasn't so great anymore after they died when she was in college. How she threw herself into her work and had just finished her residency, when she was kidnapped. She explained in detail what he had done to her.

She told them how her name used to be Lilly Swanson and that she was the only woman to escape The Cattleman Killer. She told them how she changed her name and started over in New York City. That through therapy and time, life had become somewhat normal, until a criminal had attacked her in court and all her trauma had come back to her. Starting over in Coldwater Cove had been the best decision she had made in a long time, until the copycat killer had shown up.

They were wonderful listeners and so supportive, Olivia felt good about her decision to confide in them.

"Someone must have recognized your face," Zoe said. "There's no other explanation for why they would choose a serial killer from Miami to copy."

"Exactly, but once that story hit the news, the real Cattleman Killer came out of hiding," Olivia said.

"What?" Stacy gaped at her. "Trent didn't say a word."

"Because I asked him not to. If the media finds out I'm Lilly Swanson, my life will be turned upside down all over again. I can't handle that."

"Not to mention serial killers thrive on the publicity they get," Zoe said, disgust written all over her face. "It's probably driving him crazy that no one's acknowledging him and only talking about the copycat killer."

"Has he reached out to you?" Laura asked, looking concerned.

Olivia told them about smelling the cologne in her cottage, then her underwear getting stolen and shredded, her car getting broken into, and finally the branded raccoon. She told them about the note he left in the last victim's throat, and finally about him being the one to run her off the road recently.

"No wonder Hank won't let you out of his sight." Zoe's face transformed into the tough cop Olivia had met on day one. "You can bet I'll be keeping a closer watch on you myself."

"Oh, you poor thing," Tia said. "No wonder you've been a mess lately. I would be, too. I don't know how you're keeping it all together."

"Trust me when I say I couldn't have handled any of this without you ladies being there for me, even when you didn't understand what was going on. You can't tell anyone else, but I just couldn't handle not having anyone except Hank to talk to about this anymore. As much as I adore him, I still feel like he's keeping something from me."

"Well, you're not alone anymore," Laura added. "You never were. We're your family now."

"And that means more than any of you will ever know."

* * *

"COACH CALLOWAY, how does it feel making the Little League World Series?" Stacy held out her microphone in the dugout of the Little League team's practice.

"Vindication." Derks looked straight into the camera. "I knew we would make it. Same as I know we will win the whole thing. Rosy is that good."

Stacy looked out at the field and watched Rosy strike out yet another player. "That's a lot of pressure for one athlete don't you think?" she said into the microphone and then held it toward him once more.

"Our whole team is that good," Bryce chimed in with pride. "Having a good team takes money. More money than I think any of us realized. That's why we're going to vote in a new booster club for next year. We obviously need people who can handle our funds better."

"The mismanagement of funds is a shame, really. We wanted uniforms so badly," Miley added. "This team is special. They deserve to look like rock stars while they represent Coldwater Cove to all of America."

"Well, I'm happy to tell you, the missing art was found by Deputy Granger and Jack Ross. Mayor Flemming decided to hold another art auction before the start of the series. And the proceeds are going to your team for brand new uniforms. Isn't that great?"

"That's fantastic," Miley said, her face registering shock followed by elation. "Thank you so much."

"Don't thank me. Thank your mayor."

"I know we haven't always seen eye-to-eye with the mayor, but we really do appreciate the town's support," Bryce said. "Coaches are passionate about sports and their teams, sometimes to a fault, and we apologize for that."

"I understand completely," Stacy said. "I'm not that old that I don't remember what it was like to be a young and hungry athlete. I'm just glad we were able to help. Our town could use something to lift their spirits these days, and I think your team will do exactly that.

Good luck to you and just know we'll be cheering you all on in style. Back to you, Ken."

Bryce and Miley jogged off to continue practicing with the team.

"When will this auction take place," Derks said as soon as the cameras stopped rolling and everyone was out of earshot.

"I'm not sure." Stacy tried to keep her cool. He was the only one who hadn't shown any appreciation for what her best friend was trying to do for him. He didn't care about this town. He only cared about himself and his team. "I know the mayor is finalizing the details as we speak, so it will most likely be soon."

"That's not soon enough." Derks looked agitated as he paced before her. "The mayor should have done this much sooner. Ordering new uniforms takes time. Everyone knows that. I need the money now."

"There's still plenty of time to order new uniforms. You and I both know that. How about showing a little more gratitude, like your assistant coaches, Mr. Calloway." It took everything in Stacy to remain professional. She'd never liked the guy. "The town still needs a lot of work to get back on its feet. The mayor didn't have to designate these funds to your team for uniforms. It's not like you don't have anything to wear."

He stopped pacing and glared at her with clenched fists. "How about keeping your nose out from where it doesn't belong." His face transformed into one of condescension followed by a menacing anger that seethed just beneath the surface. "I know your type. You all think you're better than me. You're not a success. You're a former athlete who could have gone somewhere but quit. A *has-been* who couldn't hack ESPN, so she came home crying to Daddy and working for small town USA."

"You don't know a thing about me." She stepped

forward, standing to her full height. One inch taller than him. "I'm not afraid of you. You're all hot air, but underneath you're nothing." She looked down her nose at him. "I pity you. I hope your team wins because the kids deserve it, but mark my words… karma is a bitch. Better cover your ass, Derks, before you get bit." She pushed past him and walked back to her news van with her head held high.

That didn't mean she didn't feel eyes full of hatred burning holes in her back with every step she took.

Maybe she should be a little afraid after all.

HANK WAS desperate to catch The Cattleman Killer as much for his own revenge as for Olivia. He told her he was falling in love with her, but the truth was, he was already head-over-heels in love with her. He hadn't wanted to scare her off, and he was terrified she would hate him for not sharing who he really was with her.

Especially after she had bared her soul to him.

But he'd worked too long and hard to put this monster away. He couldn't risk blowing that now. Any chance he had at a relationship with Olivia would have to come later. If she ever forgave him. In the meantime, he had a job to do.

He kept to the shadows behind the trio, with no one the wiser. After Hank and Trent had made their suspect list, Hank had started looking into the backgrounds of all the trios. Following them, watching, waiting for them to mess up. So far, they were all being on their best behavior, and Garcia's crew was still MIA.

Olivia was back to work and still staying with him. When she wasn't with him, she was with her friends. He felt better knowing she wasn't alone.

A movement caught Hank's eye. This trio headed down a street he didn't expect, leading right up to the

Art Museum. Maybe they were legitimately going inside. That wasn't a crime. It was the evening before the art auction, and Nolan had the recovered pieces under lock and key, with the security detail inside this time.

The trio didn't head to the front of the building.

Hank kept to the shadows and followed them all the way to the back. They were arguing, but he couldn't quite hear what they were saying. Sneaking around and acting suspicious wasn't a crime, either. Hank couldn't make his move until they broke the law.

A flash of light shined off a tire iron.

Bingo.

Hank made his move just as the perpetrator broke the seal on a window, and alarm bells went off.

"FBI, you're under arrest for breaking and entering."

Derks made a move as if to run, still holding the tire iron.

Hank raised his weapon. "I wouldn't if I were you. Drop your weapon and put your hands in the air where I can see them."

Derks did as he was told. "It's not a weapon," he grumbled.

"Really, now. A tire iron just happens to be the weapon the killer has been using around town." Hank tossed him a set of cuffs.

"K-Killer?" Miley sputtered, staring at Derks in shock, thrusting her hands high in the air. "I didn't have anything to do with this."

"Right. I think I'll stick with the facts and not your word." Hank tossed her another set of handcuffs. "Put these on and handcuff yourself, too, Bryce."

"Look, man, Derks was acting weird, so Miley and I followed him." Bryce watched her handcuff his wrist to hers with wide eyes. "When we caught him trying to break into the museum, we tried to get him to stop."

His dazed gaze met Hank's. "We're not an accessory to anything, and especially not murder."

"I was tailing you. I know exactly what you were up to." Hank kept his gun trained on them all, ready to react if necessary.

"I didn't murder anyone," Derks said. "I was here for the art, that's all."

"Why would you steal the art when it's going for an auction to buy new uniforms for our team?" Miley asked. "This doesn't make any sense."

Recognition dawned on Bryce's face. "You wanted the money for yourself. Our booster funds weren't mismanaged, were they?"

Derks looked away.

"You embezzled them," Bryce ground out. "And here I looked up to you as a coach. How could you do that to these kids?"

Miley gasped. "I-I don't know what to say."

"You don't have to say anything. It's your right to remain silent. In fact, I suggest you all get good lawyers. You're going to need them." Hank read the trio their Miranda rights as a wide-eyed Nolan appeared out back, as well as the Sheriff.

"Looks like the new alarm system works," Nolan said in disbelief as he stared at the three coaches.

"What do we have here?" Trent came to a stop by Hank.

"Breaking and entering. Attempted art theft. Most likely part of the art smuggling ring. And possibly murder."

"You're crazy." Derks looked worried for the first time. "That's all I'm going to say until I speak to my lawyer."

"Now that's the first smart thing you've said since I met you." Hank stepped back and let Trent's crew haul the trio off to jail for processing.

"Do you think he's our copycat killer?" Trent asked as he watched the cruiser pull away from the museum.

"Maybe. Maybe he's even the real deal. Anyone is capable of murder if desperate enough." Hank stared after the Sheriff's car, pondering everything that had just happened. "He looked like one desperate man to me."

* * *

LAURA HELD the art auction a couple of days later, not wanting to take a chance on any more art getting stolen. She stood in the community center, holding a press release, with a check in her hand. She stepped up to the podium, waiting for the room to quiet before speaking.

"What a rollercoaster we've been on this spring." She looked around at the packed room. Everyone had turned out for the presentation of the check to the Little League team.

"Coldwater Cove is finally getting back on her feet after the storm damage, and we have an arrest in the murders that have been happening around town. Maybe we can all finally rest easy, knowing our streets are safe again. I think what this town needs is a little good news and inspiration."

Everyone cheered.

"I am thrilled to award this check to the new co-head coaches, Bryce and Miley. They deserve it after all they've been through."

A lie detector test had proven the two assistant coaches had no clue what their head coach had been up to. And the museum's outside camera footage had con-firmed they had been trying to stop Derks from stealing the art.

It turned out Derks had a gambling addiction and

had embezzled most of their booster club funds. He owed some not-so-nice people for fronting him on bets that went south. When he ran out of money, he got desperate for more from the art sale. He pawned most of his possessions to hire a few thugs to trash the mayor's office, looking for anything to sell.

He claimed he wasn't the one who stole the art from the museum the first time, but that gave him the idea. He also claimed he didn't trash the warehouse or jump Remy, and he didn't shoot at Zoe in the woods. He didn't even own a gun.

No one believed him.

"Thank you so much, Mayor." Miley took the check from Laura. "All we've ever wanted was the best for these kids. They deserve it."

"They sure do. We're done letting them down." Bryce nodded to the audience. "And we won't let you all down, either. You can count on that."

Everyone cheered and celebrated with the team.

Larry turned the sound system on, and the band he'd recommended began to play. Betty buzzed around with Jack, distributing more food on the food tables, while Tia helped put the final touches on the decorations around the room. Given how fast she'd had to pull this off, Laura felt like all the things on her checklist had finally been checked off.

"Everything looks great, Laura." Stacy came to a stop by her.

"Thanks. I sometimes wonder how your mother kept this town together while keeping her family happy and her head on straight." Laura tucked her blonde bob behind her ears. "It's so hard sometimes."

"You're doing an amazing job. Mom would be so proud of you." Stacy hugged her. "How are things with you and Tommy?"

"Better. I finally realized if I kept waiting for things

to calm down to focus on my family, it would never happen. I'm getting better at the whole work/life balance thing."

"Good for you. Trust me, I'll be looking for some tips from you when this little one comes along." Stacy rubbed her growing stomach. Her gaze traveled across the room, and she smiled. "Look at those two."

Laura glanced over at Zoe and Jack, holding each other tight and swaying to the music. Next to them stood Olivia and Hank, deep in conversation on the edge of the dance floor. His gaze constantly roamed the room, on alert. Trent wasn't much better.

Laura frowned. "Do you think Derks is really our killer?"

"I honestly don't know what to think. After everything Olivia shared with us, The Cattleman Killer sounds like a monster. Pure evil. I hope for her sake Derks is both the copycat *and* the real killer. Because if he's not, then her nightmare has only just begun."

* * *

"Are you ready to go?" Hank tightened his arm around Olivia, pulling her closer.

Everywhere they went, he felt like he wasn't protecting her enough, especially after the clues he'd uncovered recently. She'd been through so much already, and now he felt like he was letting her down again. His stomach tightened into a knot.

Just like before.

"But we haven't even danced." She looked at him curiously with soft gray eyes that haunted his dreams.

"We can dance in my hotel room all you want," he said distractedly, still scanning his surroundings.

"Are you okay?"

He shrugged off his tension and tried for a smile

without much success. "I'm fine. I'm just worried about you, that's all."

"I appreciate that. I really do. But I'm not going to break. I have a concussion. That's all." She cupped his cheek and smiled tenderly. "I'm feeling more and more like myself every day. I promise."

He squeezed her other hand and didn't let go. "I'm not taking any chances. Derks might be the copycat, but I'm still not positive we have the original killer. Miley and Bryce weren't involved, unless Derks used some hired help. Until I have it all worked out, I want to be extra cautious."

"Okay." Olivia tightened her hand in his. She was so petite, she brought out his protective instincts something fierce. "But I'm holding you to a dance later." She winked.

"You got it." He kissed her hand, and lowered his voice, "Thank you." He led her away to say their good-byes before exiting the building.

The community center was right down the road from Coldwater Commons hotel. Hank quickly ushered Olivia into his truck and drove straight to his hotel parking lot. His eyes never stopped moving.

When he was sure they weren't followed, he guided her into his room and locked the door. He closed the blinds immediately, and then he searched every inch of the room to be sure no one was hiding there.

"So, about that dance?" Her smile came slow and sweet.

He winced, giving her an apologetic look. "Raincheck?"

"Okay, then what do you want to do? Watch a movie?" She grabbed the TV remote and clicked the TV on.

"I can't." He chose his words carefully. "I have a lead I want to follow."

"You're leaving?" Her eyes looked wide and frightened. "What's the lead?"

He hesitated a moment before replying, "I can't tell you." He reached out and took her hand in his. "Please, just trust me on this."

Her jaw fell open and a hurt expression swept over her angelic face as she slowly slipped her hand out of his. "Okay," was all she said, but he could tell he'd hurt her.

"I'll explain later. I promise. Be back soon. Don't open the door for anyone." He left without another look back before he changed his mind. But a nagging feeling in his gut told him he'd just made a decision he was going to regret.

* * *

OLIVIA SAT in the empty hotel room, wondering what just happened. Hank had left her alone, after everything he'd said about keeping her safe. Why? It didn't make sense. After all she had told him, why wouldn't he share himself with her?

He'd said he was falling in love with her.

Had he changed his mind?

She wasn't just falling in love with him. She'd known she was fully in love with him for a while now, but she didn't want to get hurt if he couldn't get there himself. What if he would never love her like she did him? She didn't think she could handle that.

Olivia thumbed through the channels and turned on a mystery movie. An hour went by without so much as a single text message. Where was he? He'd said he would be right back. She closed her eyes for what felt like only a minute, but she must have dozed off. Suddenly, she felt a presence standing over her. A smiled tipped up the corners of her lips.

"Hank," she said dreamily.

He brushed a hair back from her face, and that was all it took.

His touch was different. His skin felt different. His *smell* was different.

Her eyes flew open, and all the air in her lungs gushed out. She couldn't catch her breath. David Garcia stood over her, looking completely disheveled. She'd never seen him like this. What was he doing in Hank's hotel room?

A crazed look filled his eyes. "Hello, Lilly."

Olivia gasped and clutched her pendant cross necklace, feeling vulnerable and alone. Damn Hank for putting her in this position. She had to get her wits about her and figure out an escape plan.

"David, please, you don't have to do this." Hannah grabbed his arm, but he shrugged her hand off.

Hannah was here? Olivia thought, realizing she must be part of The Cattleman Killer's trio.

"She ruined my life. No one will hire me now," he growled, his face filling with pure hatred as he glared back at Olivia. "I recognized you the moment I saw you. The benefits of having a photographic memory."

A curse came from the doorway, and Jude walked in. Of course, he was the other part of the trio. It was all starting to make sense. The crazy intense way David always looked at Olivia, and the creepy feeling he had always given her.

"What the hell are you doing, David? You were supposed to stick to the plan and lay low after Fay." Jude tossed his hands up. "Once again, you're ruining everything we've worked so hard to create. Just like before."

"I didn't ruin anything." David reached out so quickly Olivia didn't see it coming as he grabbed a lock of her hair, tightening his fist around it. "*She* did. She couldn't leave well enough alone by poking holes in the copycat theory."

"This is all my fault." Hannah started to cry.

"It's okay." David's voice held a note of hysteria. "It'll all be okay." He nodded. "I'll fix everything. Just like before." He lifted his other hand that held a tire iron and raised it high over Olivia's head.

Olivia tightened her grip on her necklace and took a deep breath. Before she could do anything, David went flying across the room. Hannah screamed. While Jude scrambled to pick up the fallen tire iron.

"I wouldn't do that if I were you," Hank said, in a deadly voice that filled Olivia with chills.

Where had he come from at exactly the right moment?

Jude and Hannah both raised their hands high in the air, while David slowly rolled to his feet as sirens sounded off in the distance.

"I should kill you with my bare hands for what you've done. You don't deserve to live." Pure rage oozed out of every pore of Hank's body. A rage that had to do with far more than just solving a cold case. Olivia recognized that rage. She'd felt it many times herself.

For the first time, she felt like she didn't even know Hank.

"I know who you are, but you don't have a clue who I am," David sneered. "You're older and your name might be different, but I never forget a face."

"Then you know I won't stop until I avenge my sister's death. And I know exactly who you are." Hank's eyes were blazing, making him look obsessed. Nothing like the man Olivia had grown to know and love. What did his sister have to do with David?

"Including using the only living victim of The Cattleman Killer as bait?" David spat.

Olivia felt like she was going to be sick.

"It was the only way," Hank's voice sounded different. "I've been following you. I knew if I gave you an opening, you would take it. And now you're mine. I've waited five years to avenge Cindy's death."

Olivia gasped. His sister was Cindy Williams?

Cindy had been the last woman to be murdered by The Cattleman Killer, right before he'd taken Olivia. Hank had told Olivia his half-sister was from his stepfather, so of course it made sense she would have a different last name. She had been a successful young pediatrician with her whole life ahead of her, but she hadn't been as lucky as Olivia was.

Olivia had come to realize she *was* lucky.

Lucky to be alive and have the rest of her life ahead of her. She was through letting this killer rob her of anything else. Why hadn't Hank confided in her, knowing all she had been through? She of all people would have understood what he was going through and his need for revenge.

Her heart split in two.

He'd thought she would never agree to be his bait and put herself at risk of being raped again and possibly murdered this time. Why couldn't he see they were on the same page. She would have done anything to catch The Cattleman Killer and put him away once and for all, but Hank hadn't trusted her enough to take that chance. She'd thought he knew her better than that, but she'd been wrong.

He'd used her.

He didn't love her. She was a means to an end. Avenging his sister's death was more important to him than Olivia was. She sat up on the couch and straightened her clothes. That movement drew Hank's eyes to her. It was as if he just now remembered she was in the room. His face transformed from determined revenge to one of sorrow and regret.

"Olivia, I—"

"Save it." She stood.

Trent charged through the door and took in the scene before him, as Deputy Granger cuffed and arrested the trio. Hank had to fill Trent in, so Olivia took advantage of his distraction. She packed her things and returned to Trent's side when she was finished.

Trent looked back and forth between them with raised eyebrows.

"Olivia, please let me explain." Hank's eyes registered so many warring emotions: anger, frustration, grief, sorrow, regret.

She looked away, refusing to be swayed. He'd hurt her badly. "Trent, can you please drive me home?"

"Are you sure that's where you want to go, given what you've just been through?" Trent studied her closely. "I can have Stacy go with you."

Olivia was already shaking her head. "I want to go home... alone." She'd made the mistake of relying on others. Lesson learned...

From here on out, she would only rely on herself.

18

"How could I have been so stupid?" Hank paced Trent's office late that evening. They were still there, processing everything that had happened. He'd tried calling and texting Olivia, but she refused to speak to him.

"Give her time to get over the shock. Then talk to her."

"It won't matter. I hurt her. She hates me."

"Not so long ago, I felt the same way when I kept my identity from Stacy." Trent furrowed his brow. "Family is a strong motivator in making people do things they normally wouldn't. At the time, I would have done anything to clear my father's name."

"You might have kept the truth from your wife, but you never put her in harm's way." Hank shook his head, regret threatening to suffocate him. "I was so focused on catching this guy at any cost. I just never realized how big the cost would be."

"But you were there the whole time, right?" Trent pointed out, looking at him with sympathy.

"Olivia didn't know that I purposely left then doubled back and was hiding in the room across the hall, watching and waiting for Garcia to show up."

"I'm curious." Trent studied Hank. "Why did you think Garcia was The Cattleman Killer in the first place?"

"After we made our list, I've been tailing all the trios. Keeping out of sight as I logged their comings and goings. I got lucky when I recently spotted Garcia watching Olivia. I started tailing him as he tailed her." Anger filled Hank all over again. "At first, I wanted to grab him right then and there and wring his fancy neck, but I couldn't risk the case going cold again."

"That's true."

"I knew I needed to catch him in the act, so I made a plan. I was banking on him to continue to hide out and watch her, waiting for the right moment to strike. So, I knew if I set things up very carefully, I could control the situation. He would strike when and where I wanted him to, and I would be ready to make the arrest."

"Makes sense."

"It might make sense, but it doesn't lessen the blow for Olivia one bit. I should have told her about my plan, but I didn't want to worry her. And if I'm being honest, I couldn't risk her giving my plan away. For five years, I've lived and breathed The Cattleman Killer case. What he did to my sister tore my family apart. My brother is a shell of himself, and my parents have never been the same."

"Do you love Olivia?"

"I do. So damn much." Hank's heart squeezed with the realization of just how true that really was. "Should I go to her tonight? Try to talk things out?"

"That's your call, brother, but I would give her tonight to cool off. Go see her in the morning."

"You're probably right." Hank let out a breath, feeling defeated. "Thanks, Trent. You've become a good friend. I just pray Olivia will forgive me, and it's not too late for us. I honestly don't know what I'll do if I lose her."

* * *

OLIVIA SET her cell phone on the counter, ignoring yet another text message from Hank. She wasn't ready to talk to him and wasn't sure when or if she would ever be. She poured herself a glass of red wine and walked out back to sit on her patio. She hadn't been back here since the incident with the branded raccoon in her kitchen.

Now that the killer was caught, she was through living her life in fear.

Hank had taught her how to love again. She would always be grateful to him for that, but she couldn't trust him with her heart anymore. He would most likely go back to Boston. As much as she loved Coldwater Cove and would miss her new friends, she was considering moving on to someplace new to truly start over this time, with no more fear hanging over her head, and no more bad memories.

It was late, but she wasn't ready to sleep yet. Waves gently rolled into the shoreline, the sound soothing to her frazzled nerves. She looked up at the sky. No clouds, with stars so bright it took her breath away. She was going to be okay. The bad guys were gone. Her stomach turned over into a knot. So, why did one thought keep nagging at her brain?

David Garcia didn't smell right.

She would never forget that unmistakable pungent cologne the real Cattleman Killer had worn for as long as she lived. Maybe he only wore it during a kill, but another thought bothered her. While David's voice had been menacing, it wasn't the same sinister sneer that had chilled her to the bone five years ago and in every nightmare since.

She was probably just being paranoid. After years of paranoia, it was going to take a while before she didn't second guess everything. She took another sip of her wine, but then the world stopped around her. She dropped her glass and watched it shatter all over the patio, red wine staining the surface like blood all over again.

The smell was back!

Her whole body vibrated with terror, and her scream lodged in her throat.

"Hello, Lilly," hissed a voice she would *never* forget.

Acid hit her throat. It was *him*. The *real* Cattleman Killer.

She surged to her feet, clutched her necklace, and spun around to face him, but he was ready for her. The last thing she saw before he slipped a burlap sack over her head was a man in a dark raincoat wearing a ski mask.

He quickly tied her hands and dragged her out front of her cottage. She couldn't see anything as he threw her in the trunk of a vehicle.

"You're going to drag us down with you if you go through with this," said another man's muffled voice.

"You promised you would behave. I don't understand why you have these urges," a woman said, her voice hard to hear as well through the trunk.

Olivia didn't know where they were taking her. All she knew for certain, was that history was about to repeat itself, and this time she wouldn't make it out alive if she didn't do something. She clutched her necklace and closed her eyes as she thought of her parents.

"Don't you worry, Mom and Dad. This time I'm ready."

* * *

STACY WENT to work bright and early the next morning. The news station was buzzing with energy. With all the arrests, there were a few stories that needed wrapping up. She was just glad none of them were in danger anymore. She placed a hand over her stomach. The stress was getting to her.

Trent had told her the night before what had happened between Hank and Olivia. Stacy, more than anyone, could understand how Olivia felt. To put your trust in someone fully, only to have them lie to you, was devastating. She'd tried to reach out to her, but Olivia hadn't answered. Stacy left a message, telling her she was there for her day or night if she needed her, but she understood if she needed some time alone. She only hoped Olivia could look objectively at the facts later and understand why Hank had felt compelled to keep her in the dark.

"You're all set, Mrs. West." Larry slipped a tool back into his toolbox.

"You're a life saver, Larry. We don't need audio problems when the biggest news stories in years have hit our town."

"You shouldn't have any more problems." He nodded once. "I'm just glad I can finally take some time off."

"Oh yeah? Any fun plans?" She grinned.

He flushed pink then cleared his throat. "I have a couple friends I'm going to spend a few days with."

"That's great! Where are you going?"

"A little fishing spot nearby, but don't worry. I'll have my phone on if any emergencies happen. You can count on that."

"Can I give you a word of advice?"

"Sure." He looked at her curiously.

"Unplug. Enjoy yourself. You work too hard. No one's as good as you are, but I'm sure we can get by if the need arises. Deal?"

"Deal." Larry left, a little lighter in his steps.

Stacy smiled. He really was such a nice man. She noticed Winston waiting by the door, so she walked over to him. He was saying something out loud, but no one was around. She came to a stop beside him, and he looked up at her startled.

She smiled. "Talking to yourself?"

His eyes widened and then he flushed slightly, clearing his voice.

"Don't worry, I do it all the time." She winked. "Which angle to take for a story I'm working on. Debates I'm trying to win against my husband. Solving the world's problems." She laughed. "You know, everyday stuff."

"Exactly." He nodded. "Who better to hash things out with than ourselves?"

"Right?"

"Hash what out?" Lorelai walked through the door and stood by his side.

"Whether we should have French or Italian for dinner tonight." Winston's smile came slow and sweet as he stared at Lorelai like he'd rather have her for dinner.

"French, of course, love. With dessert at my place." Lorelai blew him a kiss.

"Now there's a sight I'd never thought I would see." Stacy raised an eyebrow. "Still sharing notes?"

"Something like that." Winston chuckled, undoing the top button of his shirt as if suddenly warm.

"I've been replaced so quickly." Stacy laughed.

"We're having fun, darling, but make no mistake. He's still very much my competitor." Lorelai smiled all catlike.

"I love a challenge." Winston winked, and then looked at Stacy with sincerity in his eyes and tone. "It's been a pleasure working with you, Stacy." He held out his hand and shook hers. "You're good. Are you sure we can't steal you for bigger things?"

"Not a chance. I love Coldwater Cove, but good luck to you both on the anchor positions."

They nodded their thanks.

"Care to share a cab to the airport?" he asked Lorelai.

"I thought you'd never ask." She took his arm and the two left.

Stacy was about to look over her story notes when her cell phone rang. She glanced at the caller ID and smiled tenderly. "Hey, hon. Miss me already?"

"Always," Trent said, but the tone of his voice had her smile vanishing.

"What's wrong?"

"Hank went to talk to Olivia this morning, but she wasn't there."

"Maybe she left town to clear her head."

"That's what I thought at first, until Hank told me her wine glass was shattered all over the patio... that's not the worst of it."

Stacy swallowed hard, knowing in her gut what he was going to tell her. "What else could possibly be worse?"

"There was a piece of burlap on the ground."

Fear clogged Stacy's throat and it took her a minute to speak. "Oh, God," her voice hitched, "he's got her again, Trent!"

"I know, hon, but don't panic. I'm on my way to meet Hank at the community center to organize a search party."

"I'll be there in a minute."

"Maybe you shouldn't—"

"It's my job, Trent."

"I know, I know. But I don't have to like it."

She was beginning to understand how Laura felt and the struggle she would be faced with once the baby came along, but she couldn't worry about that now. "There's one more thing to consider."

"What's that?"

"Olivia doesn't drink during the day. He had to have taken her last night. That's a big head start. What if we're too late, Trent?"

"We can't think like that. Stay positive, but you're right. We'd better get going. The first forty-eight hours are crucial."

* * *

HANK STOOD beside Trent in the community center, still in shock. "I should have listened to my gut and gone to talk to Olivia last night."

"If you had gone to see her, the killer wouldn't have struck," Trent said. "He would have watched and waited for another moment to make his move."

"I shouldn't have let her leave me." Hank forced back the emotion threatening to suffocate him.

"You couldn't force her to stay. The important thing is, you're here now. Stay strong. She needs you now more than ever. We're going to get this guy. He's arrogant. He's not going to run. He's going to choose a place in the woods right here, so he can rub it in our face how good he is. Only a coward runs, and he's not that."

Hank inhaled a deep breath and focused. "You're right. Let's think about what we know. He likes to put his victims in an abandoned shack, but he's smart. He won't use the same place twice, so the location he killed Ali in is a waste of time to search."

"Agreed, but I don't want to take any chances. I have Larry checking out that location just to be sure."

"Larry?" Stacy asked, joining her husband. "I just saw him at the news station. He told me he was going away for a couple of days with friends."

"He was, but he heard the news over his police scanner."

Hank raised a brow.

Trent shrugged as he continued. "It's a hobby of his. Anyway, he came back to help. I had already designated other areas to be searched, so I figured it couldn't hurt to make sure the killer's not at that location."

"Is everyone else set on where they're going?" Hank hovered over a map spread out on a table in the middle of the community center.

Most of the town was there, which showed just how much everyone loved Olivia. If... no, *when*... they got out of this, he was going to lay it all on the line and tell her how much he loved her and that he would spend the rest of his life making things up to her. He planned to cherish her forever, if only she would give him the chance.

"Remy, Jack, and Zoe head up the coast and enter the woods where you found the art," Trent said, looking at the three of them for clarification.

They all nodded.

"Tia, Calvin, and Dijon, you can check out all the cabins you have on your books that are located in the woods."

They all nodded.

"The rest of you divide up into groups between the town council members, sugar shack farmers, and hunters. They know where all the shacks and cabins that aren't listed on the books are located."

Everyone started pairing off into groups with people they knew.

"What about me?" Nolan asked.

"Larry hasn't left yet. Why don't you partner up with him in case he needs backup," Trent said.

"I don't know much about backing anyone up, but I'm happy to help in any way." Nolan headed off to find Larry.

"Winston, what on earth are you doing?" Stacy said, as he and Lorelai came to a stop beside her.

"We couldn't let you have all the fun, now, could we?" Winston said.

"We got wind of what was going on from one of my sources before we even reached the airport," Lorelai added. "How can we help?"

"You can tag along with Trent, Hank, and me."

"I appreciate that, Stacy," Winston said. "If you ever need a recommendation for anything, don't hesitate to ask."

She nodded. "Thanks."

"Okay, everyone, daylight is wasting." Hank picked up his supplies. "If you see or hear anything, shoot off your flare. Stay alert and be ready, people. This is no amateur we're dealing with."

19

OLIVIA SAT in the corner of an abandoned shack, cold and alone. Her leggings and t-shirt were ripped but still very much on, thank God. The Cattleman Killer seemed different this time. More frazzled. Rusty. Or maybe it was because she was older and wiser this time around. More relaxed from the wine. More determined from her frustration with Hank. Whatever the reason, she felt bold and unafraid.

The killer didn't like that she wasn't falling to pieces like before.

As soon as he'd thrown her into the cabin, he'd tied her hands to a hook on the wall and yanked the burlap sack off her head. He still wore his ski mask as he reached for her shirt, but then his phone rang. He cursed and seemed agitated as he stepped outside. He still refused to let her see his accomplices. She heard the three of them argue through the cabin wall, saying something about laying a few traps, and then there was silence for the rest of the night.

That had given Olivia time to form a plan.

Coldwater Cove was smaller than Miami, and she had more people in her corner here, making her odds of survival better. She had to trust her gut that Hank would keep trying to call her. At the latest, he would wait until morning to go see her. When he saw her phone and the broken glass, he would know someone had taken her.

She just had to stay alive until then and come up with a trap of her own.

* * *

HANK STUDIED the map he'd brought with him, marking off each spot that had been cleared. They'd been searching all morning, and he was trying not to get discouraged with each passing hour of dead ends. Each group kept radioing in with locations to be marked off. They'd started wide and were narrowing their search inland.

"Sheriff West here," Trent answered his cell phone.

They all stopped walking and looked at him, waiting for more news.

"Roger that." Trent hung up. "That makes three people injured in boobytraps so far. None of them life threatening."

"Thank goodness for that," Stacy said.

"Whoever this is obviously has knowledge of the woods and survival skills," Winston said.

"That could be just about anyone around these parts," Lorelai added, lifting her hand to shield her eyes and search the area.

"That's true," Hank said. "I've looked into all of the residents of The Cove and many of the visiting tourists over the course of the investigation. So many of them are hunters, former Eagle Scouts, ex-military."

"Which makes our job that much harder," Trent said, when his cell phone rang again. "West here." Trent listened, his face frowning. "Copy that. I'll let the groups know to be on the lookout." Trent hung up and sent several group messages before speaking.

"What happened now?" Stacy asked.

"Nolan got separated from Larry." Trent looked at Hank. "A bear surprised them, and Larry said Nolan whipped out a gun and took him down with a single shot."

"I didn't know Nolan owned a gun," Stacy said.

Hank narrowed his eyes. "So much for not liking guns and not being very good at backing anyone up?"

"Exactly." Trent nodded. "Something tells me he's not lost. The question is, where's he headed?"

"Only one way to find out," Winston said. "We keep moving."

"Winston, look out!" Lorelai yelled.

Too late.

Winston's eyes sprang wide in shock, and he yelped in pain as the net he'd stepped into snagged around his ankle and yanked him upside down. He cursed as he swung back and forth, looking embarrassed in front of Lorelai.

"Hang in there, Winston," Stacy said. "Trent and Hank are working on cutting you down."

"I've got you." Trent steadied Winston.

Hank used a knife to cut the rope that would release him. "Are you hurt?" he asked the reporter as he tumbled to the ground with Trent helping to break his fall.

"Just my pride." Winston's face was flushed red as he stood and dusted himself off. "I can make it through a war zone in one piece, but I apparently can't make it through the woods of Maine unscathed."

"We all have our mishaps, darling. You're fine." Lorelai started walking. "We'd better get a move on."

"Yes, good idea." Winston followed at a slower pace, scanning every inch of the ground before each careful step he took.

Hank appreciated the man's help, but they were never going to reach Olivia before nightfall at this rate. He glanced at the darkening sky and didn't like the looks of those gray clouds. "You all have maps and radios. Why don't we split up. We'll cover more ground that way."

"Good idea," Trent said. "I just got a text from Zoe. Apparently, Remy got separated from them as well. We now have three missing persons to look for." Trent pulled out his map. "Stacy and I will head here." He pointed to a spot. "Winston and Lorelai, you head here." He pointed to another spot. "Hank, you're on your own, but I trust you can handle that."

"Roger that." Hank nodded once, preferring to be on his own, then headed in his direction double-time. *I'm coming for you, princess. Just hold on a little longer.*

* * *

OLIVIA WAS CONFUSED. Five years ago, the killer had never left her alone this long. She hadn't seen him since the night before. She'd really expected him and his accomplices to show up by now. Her growling stomach told her it had to be getting near dinner time. He never fed her food, but he at least used to give her water.

Tugging on her restraints once more, to no avail, she cried out in frustration just to hear another voice. The wind had picked up and was howling through the cracks of the shack. She sat there for what felt like another hour, the rain falling steadily now and leaking through the shack's roof.

Footsteps sounded outside.

She held her breath.

"Olivia? Are you in there?" a woman's voice asked. "It's Lorelai."

Olivia wilted with relief. "Y-Yes," she cried out.

"Hang on," a man said. "It's Winston. The door's locked. I'm looking for something to pry it open."

"Oh, my God, look Winston," Lorelai said. "He left the tire iron."

Several moments later, the sound of wood splintering happened seconds before the door popped open, the rusted lock falling to the ground. Winston and Lorelai ran into the room, soaking wet. They pushed back their hoods and rushed over to her.

"Oh, you poor thing, you must be freezing." Lorelai took off her coat and wrapped it around Olivia's shoulders.

"I'm just so glad you guys found me." Olivia sobbed.

"Do we have anything in the supply bag to cut these ties, Lorelai?" Winston asked, taking off his own coat and draping it over Olivia's legs. "We need to hurry before the killer comes back."

Lorelai rummaged through their supply bag, found a pair of scissors and handed them to Winston. He started cutting the ropes on Olivia's wrists to set her free. A whooshing noise sounded, and they both looked toward the shack door.

Lorelai stepped back inside and shut the door to the keep the rain out. "I just shot off the flair to signal Sheriff West and Agent Masters. The whole town is out looking for you."

"Good idea," Winston said. "We should probably move out of here, though. What if the killer comes back before someone finds us?"

"Good point," Lorelai said. "Can you walk?" she asked Olivia.

Olivia nodded, struggling to her feet. Her body was stiff from the position she'd been in all night and all day. They took a couple steps toward the cabin door, when the unmistakable sound of more footsteps came from outside.

They all stepped back as the doorknob began to turn.

Larry walked in and locked eyes with Olivia, carrying a ski mask in his hand and a burlap sack in the other.

Olivia gasped, her heart sinking.

Winston didn't hesitate. He jumped on Larry, knocking him to the ground. The men struggled, until Larry managed to scramble free. He pulled a gun, cornering Olivia, Lorelai, and Winston against the far wall.

"What the hell is wrong with you?" Larry asked.

"Me?" Winston sputtered. "You're the one holding a ski mask and burlap sack."

"I found them in the woods, and then I saw your flare," Larry added.

"That's a likely story," Lorelai said.

"You can't seriously think I have anything to do with this, do you?" Larry turned his questioning gaze on Olivia.

Olivia didn't know what to think. The bag had something inside of it. She could tell by the way that it drooped. "What's inside the bag?" she asked in lieu of answering his question.

Larry's eyes never left Olivia's as he pulled out an ancient bottle of liquid. A homemade, one-of-a-kind men's cologne.

Olivia gagged. She would know that smell anywhere.

Suddenly, Hank came running through the door with his weapon drawn, pointing it at Larry. "Don't move, Shaw. Winston and Lorelai, come over by me." They did as he told them. His eyes never left Larry's as he asked, "You okay, Olivia?"

She thought about that and was surprised when she realized she *was* okay. Hank had never looked so good to her. He hadn't actually lied to her; he just hadn't told her everything. She understood what it was like to want revenge for so long. Frankly, she didn't care about any of that anymore. He was alive. She was alive. And they loved each other. All she wanted to do was hold him, but she didn't want to distract him.

"I'm fine," she said with confidence, and his posture told her that was all he needed to hear. "That's the right ski mask and cologne. Winston and Lorelai rescued me, but then Larry showed up before we could get away."

"This is not how it looks. I can promise you that," Larry said carefully. "I am *not* The Cattleman Killer."

"No, *I* am," hissed a voice so evil it had them all turning around in circles.

A man's voice, a woman's voice, the killer's voice…

No one else had come into the shack.

Everything happened at once. Changing voices, wrestling bodies, and a gun went off.

"Now I have two of you to play with," hissed the killer's voice.

"Please, Dev, it's not worth it. Can we just go now? We'll start over again. Just the three of us," said a woman's voice.

"Shut up, Ang. We all can't be good like you. Frankly, I don't want to be. You're boring," hissed the killer's voice again.

"I've never asked you for anything, Dev. I've let you have all the others, but I really like this one. Please don't hurt her," said another man's voice.

Olivia stared in disbelief.

There were three distinct voices, but only one person left standing in the shack, holding two guns and talking to himself. Hank lay unconscious on the floor, bleeding from a bullet wound. Larry lay groaning against the wall, holding his head. And Lorelai cowered beside Olivia in the corner, bruised and bleeding. The

Cattleman Killer wasn't a trio. That left only one possibility...

Winston Bass had a multiple personality disorder.

Lorelai looked like she was going to be sick.

All of the voices had come from Winston's mouth, his facial expressions and physical movements mirroring whichever character was speaking at the moment. Olivia knew if they were all going to make it out of this alive, she had to be brave. She couldn't let him tie them up. She had to fight back. She got to her feet slowly, keeping a whimpering Lorelai behind her.

"Winston, are you in there?" Olivia asked calmly. "It's me, Olivia."

Winston looked at her confused for a moment.

"You don't want to hurt me, do you?" she continued, with a tone she'd heard her therapist use.

"No, never. I've never wanted to hurt anyone, but the Devil makes me do it." Winston looked sorry, his hands shaking. "I hate the Devil. He's so mean."

His face suddenly turned serene, and his voice raised several octaves as he waved the guns about in a feminine way. "I don't like Dev, either. I tried to get him to stop, but he won't listen to either of us, right, Winston?"

His movements stilled once more as the angel within him transformed back into Winston. "Right, Ang. Dev never listens to either of us," Winston agreed in his normal voice, looking forlorn as he stared at Lorelai apologetically. "I'm so sorry, Lor. I really did like you. I should have known he would never let me keep you. The Devil's selfish. Always wanting all the women for himself."

"I'm listening," Olivia said, trying to get Winston to focus on her. "I see you, Winston. I *hear* you. If you let us go, we won't tell anyone. Therapy might help you."

His face suddenly twisted into one she didn't recognize, his eyes darkening into the same evil ones she'd seen glaring at her through a ski mask. He didn't look like Winston as he gripped the guns with deadly confidence. "We don't need help. There's nothing wrong with us. We're perfect the way we are, and you're not going anywhere, Lilly," Dev hissed, cocking the weapons. "It's time I finished what I started. I'm only sorry we don't have time to play first."

Olivia steadied her feet and clutched the cross pendent around her neck, thrusting her chin up a notch. "I'm not afraid of you this time."

"You should be." He took a step forward and pointed the gun at her.

"A gun, really? You're obviously afraid of barely five-foot me." Her heart was pounding, but she was banking on his ego taking a hit.

He scowled, shoving the guns in the waistband of his jeans. "I'm the Devil. I'm not afraid of anyone. I'm going to enjoy strangling the life out of you. Maybe it will be my new MO since someone tried to steal my other one." Raising his hands, he slowly walked over to her.

Olivia didn't flinch or step away.

With a crazed look in his eyes, he lunged for her. As if in slow motion, muscle memory kicked in from five years of practicing this move. She pulled a dagger from a hidden compartment inside her cross pendant and swung it up, directly across the carotid artery in his neck as she ducked and rolled out of the way at the same time. His arms closed around air as he fell to the ground, staring at her with shock and disbelief as the life drained out of his eyes.

She fell to the floor, sobbing. She'd taken her power back, and her nightmare was finally over.

EPILOGUE

"You look great in that uniform, my handsome boyfriend," Olivia said to Hank as he stopped into her office before heading to his down the hall. She sat behind her brand-new desk. The room looked totally different, filled with plants, colors... life.

That wasn't the only thing that was different. Her hair hung loose in a fun, flirty bob. The first thing she'd done when she got back to town was cut her hair and donate it to other women in need. It had served its purpose in shielding her, but now she was free.

Hank bent down and kissed her softly on the lips. "Why thank you, my beautiful girlfriend." He winked. "I love you."

She kissed his cheek. "I love you more."

He kissed her forehead. "I love you most."

She sighed in pure happiness. "Not possible."

She'd finally gone through and fully organized Clive's Catastrophe, making it her own because she'd decided to stay in town. She'd made real friends who were now her family, and had learned how hard that was to come by. No way was she giving that up. With the new money the town had raised, they had the funds to pay her for her new title as the official Medical Examiner of Coldwater Cove, instead of just the coroner.

Hank had recovered from his bullet wound and had decided to become the new Chief of Police. The mayor had suggested Trent and Hank had worked so well together, that The Cove could benefit from their very own additional police force. Hank had agreed, having a pretty strong motivation to settle down now that the real Cattleman Killer was dead.

"Tia has a new rental house for us to look at after work," Olivia said, "if you're available." It turned out Tia, Calvin, and Dijon really were just realtors, which Olivia was thrilled about because Tia had become one of her closest friends.

Hank tapped his badge. "See this chief badge? It comes with some perks. I'm always available for you."

"I'm gonna hold you to that." She blew him a kiss. "I can't get over how much things have changed in The Cove so quickly."

"I know. I still can't believe Remy and Nolan were the ones behind the art smuggling ring, but it makes sense. They staged the first museum break-in to make Nolan look innocent and the marina warehouse break-in to make Remy look innocent. It was a brilliant cover."

"Exactly," Olivia agreed. "It makes perfect sense that when Zoe and Jack went back for the art by boat, Remy tipped Nolan off. He was the one who had shot at her three times from the shore. I mean, according to Trent, the man proved to be an expert marksman when he saved Larry from the bear."

"No kidding." Hank shook his head. "Apparently, when Nolan wandered off from Larry during the search and rescue mission for you, Remy also wandered off from Jack and Zoe. He met up with Nolan to move the last of the hidden art before one of the rescue teams could find it. Unfortunately for them, Zoe is very good at her job and foiled their plans."

"I'm not surprised she wanted the new harbormaster position," Oliva added with a wistful smile. "I'm so happy for her. She loves the water more than anything else, except Jack, maybe. I was also relieved Larry really is just a maintenance man. He's so good, and this town can't afford to lose all its new people. Not to mention, I really liked him."

"Oh, Larry's good, all right. He's an ex-military badass maintenance man who's agreed to help both Trent and me out on occasion, should the need arise."

"That's amazing," Olivia said. "What's the latest on David, Hannah, and Jude?"

"They're awaiting trial for several crimes." Hank frowned. "Their situation was such an unnecessary tragedy."

"I know… poor Fay. I still can't believe she died by accident."

"Jealousy can make people do crazy things. David was having an affair with Fay, but still stringing Hannah along after promising he would break things off with all the others. Hannah caught them together, and that was the last straw. She lost her cool for one senseless second and shoved Fay in a jealous rage. Fay hit her head and died."

"Things would have gone so much better for them if they had just called the police right then and there."

"That's true, but then I never would have met you." Hank's gaze softened on her.

Olivia's insides warmed with pleasure. "I never thought of it that way, but I believe our paths would have crossed at some point. Neither of us was going to rest easy until The Cattleman Killer was no longer a threat."

"I like that. We were fated to be together. The

Garcia gang just sped things along. I guess Jude was in a panic over what to do, insisting they not go to the police and try to cover it up instead. David, having a photographic memory, recognized you right away and decided to make it look like the work of The Cattleman Killer, thinking that would keep all suspicion off them."

"Little did he know, he had a few details wrong," Olivia pointed out. "He didn't expect me to declare him a copycat killer."

"That's what drew the real Cattleman Killer out of hiding as soon as Winston saw the news story. His alter ego, the Devil, couldn't handle someone trying to be him, no matter how much the angel within him tried to get him to behave. There are actually many serial killers who have DID."

"DID?"

"Dissociative Identity Disorder, more commonly known in the past as Multiple Personality Disorder. It happens when there have been cognitive splits in a person's mind, normally in response to some kind of trauma. It's the mind's way of preserving itself. When the person gets triggered, they simply create a different identity to deal with the issue."

"Do you think Winston's traumatic event was when he snapped and killed his fiancé after she left him?" Olivia was just trying to make sense of how someone like Winston could turn into such a monster.

"Probably so. Murder was too traumatic for Winston to fathom, so this Devil identity split off to be someone who validated murder and didn't see it as bad. Dev sees himself as justified and has his own set of rules. Winston is just an accomplice. He knows Dev is doing the killing, but he is too afraid to stop him and get in trouble. He allows himself to be pushed out easily to run away and let Dev take over. The Angel identity was probably created because Winston needed good to deal with the evil. Ang gave him hope that he too was a good person."

"I'm so glad I got therapy right away." Olivia shivered. "It's not too far-fetched to think I might have created a different identity to deal with the trauma I went through."

"You're an amazing woman, Liv, and I'm so grateful to have you in my life." He smiled at her with such tenderness, but then his smiled slipped. "I just wish I would have seen the signs in Winston... then you wouldn't have had to go through any more trauma. I really thought there were three separate people involved."

"So did everyone."

"Like Garcia, Winston also recognized you right away when he came to town, but I think he knew he had to bide his time before he could make his move. He did stir things up by mentioning the art smuggling ring up the coast, sending good ole Nolan and Remy into a frenzy to get rid of their stockpile before getting caught."

"Poor Lorelai is still in therapy. I'm not sure she'll ever be the same." Olivia shook her head. "I can't believe Winston went to all that trouble to set those traps, and even trigger one to keep the suspicion off of himself."

"I'm just glad we won't ever have to worry about that monster again. You and me together, forever, with no more secrets. We survived," Hank said.

"No, we *thrived*." Olivia ran her fingertips down the cross pendant around her neck, giving thanks and sending a kiss up to heaven. Her prayers had been answered.

She was no longer alone.

ABOUT THE AUTHOR

Kari Lee Townsend is a National Bestselling Author of mysteries & a tween superhero series. She also writes romance and women's fiction as Kari Lee Harmon. With a background in English education, she's now a full-time writer, wife to her own superhero, mom of 3 sons, 1 darling diva, 1 daughter-in-law & 2 lovable fur babies. These days you'll find her walking her dogs or hard at work on her next story, living a blessed life.

ALSO BY THE AUTHOR

A Touch of Malice (Kalli Ballas Mystery #3)

Two Cents of Doom (Kalli Ballas Mystery #2)

Mind Over Murder (Kalli Ballas Mystery #1)

Harmful Habits (Cece Monroe Mystery #1)

Murder in the Meditation (Sunny Meadows Mystery #8)

Chaos and Cold Feet (Sunny Meadows Mystery short story #7)

Hazard in the Horoscope (Sunny Meadows Mystery #6)

Perish in the Palm (Sunny Meadows Mystery #5)

Shenanigans in the Shadows (Sunny Meadows Mystery short story #4)

Trouble in the Tarot (Sunny Meadows Mystery #3)

Corpse in the Crystal Ball (Sunny Meadows Mystery #2)

Tempest in the Tea Leaves (Sunny Meadows Mystery #1)

Rise of the Phenoteens (Digital Diva #2)

Talk to the Hand (Digital Diva #1)

Dangerous Thaw (Coldwater Cove #3)

Frozen Waters (Coldwater Cove #2)

Dark Seas (Coldwater Cove #1)

Valley of Secrets

Until Tomorrow

Jingle all the Way (Merry Scroog-mas novella #3)

Sleigh Bells Ring (Merry Scroog-mas novella #2)

Naughty or Nice (Merry Scroog-mas novella #1)

Brook (Lakehouse Treasures novella #4)
Meghan (Lakehouse Treasure novella #3)
Amber (Lakehouse Treasures novella #2)
James (Lakehouse Treasures novella #1)

Sleeping in the Middle (Comfort Club #1)

Love Lessons
Project Produce

Spurred by Fate (Triple R Ranch short story #2)
Destiny Wears Spurs (Triple R Ranch #1)

Frozen Waters (Coldwater Cove #2)
Dark Seas (Coldwater Cove #1)

Valley of Secrets
Until Tomorrow

Jingle all the Way (Merry Scroog-mas novella #3)
Sleigh Bells Ring (Merry Scroog-mas novella #2)
Naughty or Nice (Merry Scroog-mas novella #1)

Brook (Lakehouse Treasures novella #4)
Meghan (Lakehouse Treasure novella #3)
Amber (Lakehouse Treasures novella #2)
James (Lakehouse Treasures novella #1)

Sleeping in the Middle (Comfort Club #1)

Love Lessons
Project Produce